A Rogue's Tales

The Ties That Bind

by
Robert A. Lancaster

Order this book online at www.trafford.com
or email orders@trafford.com

Most Trafford titles are also available at major online book retailers.

Note for Librarians: A cataloguing record for this book is available from Library and Archives Canada at www.collectionscanada.ca/amicus/index-e.html

Printed in Victoria, BC, Canada.

ISBN: 978-1-4269-1363-1

Our mission is to efficiently provide the world's finest, most comprehensive book publishing service, enabling every author to experience success. To find out how to publish your book, your way, and have it available worldwide, visit us online at www.trafford.com

Trafford rev. 09/11/09

North America & international
toll-free: 1 888 232 4444 (USA & Canada)
phone: 250 383 6864 ♦ fax: 812 355 4082

I here by dedicate (this attempt at writing)

To

Todd/Wayne/Bill & just forgot your names

Who kept me up on weekends arguing over where to go in town.
Then tricked me into joining.

Carr's life, so far...

With a pair of, strangely strong moralled thief parents to raise him, Carr was given a better life than most. A quiet childhood on a simple farm deep in the Tau woodlands, and taught many of life's skills.

Hal, a half elf and family friend provided much knowledge on the lands, plants and animals around him.

Several winters spent in the farm house with a scholar, Jacob, learning to read and write.

One spring traveling to the town of Ingleside with his father and the scholar, they met up with an untrustworthy goblin thief, Uoto Gutoo in the village of Ahn. Wanting to join their trek, mainly to discuss a proposition with Alfred, Carr's father.

Keeping Carr out of the conversation, Jacob, got Carr to chat about the woodland creatures seen. Talking way too much about rats Jacob noted, in jest, how much Carr had in common with them. Small and hairy, always scurrying about in search of food, lurking in the shadows and hiding in small spaces. Finding it amusing and being young Carr agreed, occasionally squeaking as the walked.

The conversation soured between Alfred and Uoto. Alfred wanted nothing to do with Uoto's plan.

Starting to cross a narrow wooden bridge Uoto became angry and frustrated knocking Carr aside to hastily get away from Alfred.

Carr was knocked off the bridge into a fast moving stream. Torn between wanting to kill Uoto and save Carr, Alfred only yelled at the goblin.

Taking opposite sides of the stream Alfred and Jacob chase after Carr.

Annoyed at all and tired of the young boy squeaking away for the last league Uoto yelled back. "Rats can swim." Continuing on to Ingleside.

Fortunately Carr could swim, struggling some he made it to the bank.

Glad to see the boy is okay, Jacob chuckles calling out from the other side. "You can toss rats into raging waters and they still manage to find shore."

From that moment on Alfred and Jacob started calling the boy the orcish name for rats, Carr.

Finding Carr good for traveling with Alfred slowly began teaching the young boy, skills, skills of a thief. Despite mother's disapproval, he picked it up quickly and wished to learn more.

Soon the innocent trips to local villages and towns turned into jobs, that mother wasn't pleased with.

Wanting a better life for Carr mother stated her case getting Alfred to stop taking him on ventures. Even if they were just to retrieve lost items within barren caves or ruins.

But it was too late the desire for adventure had been set into Carr's mind and soul.

After a long debate and realizing that he'll not stay on the farm forever mother made a serious request. If taking on the life of his parent's past, he should learn how to properly fight.

At the age of eleven Carr is taken to meet with Hal. Informing the half elf of the intent for the boy's future he hesitantly agrees to take Carr to meet with a Master Fighter.

Across the mountains Hal and Carr trekked, reaching a secluded castle ruin. Inside Carr was introduced to a serious man of few words, Braccus.

Hearing the skills already acquired and to what Carr plans to do with them, Braccus gets into a long conversation with Hal, smartly Carr sits quietly.

Not wanting to train a future thief, Braccus is impressed at how still and quiet Carr remains.

After a few days of training Braccus sees something worthy in Carr's character and said to Hal. "He'll never be a great warrior, but perhaps something better than a common thief."

Deciding to see what he can get out of Carr, Braccus takes him on as a student.

Two years of training are put into Carr and on a late fall visit from Hal, Carr is released. Braccus figures he's learned enough, not all, but enough.

Back on the farm Carr's youthful urges want to put his new skills to test. Mother reluctantly allows him to venture with his father.

The following summer Carr goes to visit with Hal also hoping of spending time with a pretty female neighbor, Sonja.

Arriving in Ahn Carr finds Hal, with another favored family friend Violetta, a healer. Both headed north to help out villages caught amongst wars with King Darvel. Bored Carr wanted to go, Violetta seeing him still as a boy said no.

Hiding within their cart of supplies Carr sneaks away. Found a few days later, too far to go back Hal defends Carr and promised to watch over him.

At the same time Alfred decided to take on a job, to which became his demise.

Now the man of the family Carr does his best to keep the farm going and his mother happy.

However the need for adventure slowly gets the better of him. Starting from taking on simple quests while in the villages, to taking off for weeks at a time searching for treasure and coin.

Upsetting his mother more and more as she sits in the secluded farmhouse, wondering where he is and if he's still alive.

At fifteen, Carr becomes bolder with his jobs interfering and affecting merchants. The merchants raise their concerns of troublesome trading within the open territory of the Tau woodlands to their King Darvel.

Curious of the Tau woodlands and not yet part of his territory King Darvel sent a group to survey the lands and towns.

This traveling party was too tempting for Carr's curiosity. Deciding to sneak in and steal what he can from the group as they slept was Carr's worst mistake.

Only getting away with a small amount of coin and some maps, Carr thought it easy and fun. King Darvel found it as a personal attack. Sending out horsemen to route out thieves, bandits and anyone else found to be questionable in nature.

By the next year Darvel was sending out a party of armed men to collect taxes, with force if needed. No village was to be missed in their routes.

While out adventuring in the fall of his seventeenth year Carr left his mother alone one too many times. Darvel's tax collecting party headed south from Ahn. Reaching only the Great Swamp they turned back, coming across an unseen path heading east.

Three of the tax collector's horsemen were sent to investigate the path. They of course came across the farm and a lone woman.

Inviting themselves inside the farmhouse they noticed several nice weapons. The kind no farmer can afford. Stating their business and intent Carr's mother told them she had no coin to give. Not believing her, the men ransack the farmhouse: Taking the most valuable items and before leaving informing her that they'll be back next year.

Returning home Carr finds a very upset mother and home. Always feeling bad for not being there for his father in the end and now his mother's safety in danger, Carr truly wants to do right by his mother.

Finding out what happened and what was taken Carr vows to make it right to her. She of course just wants him to forget about it and to make it right with her by helping her on the farm.

He just can't let the invasion of his home go.

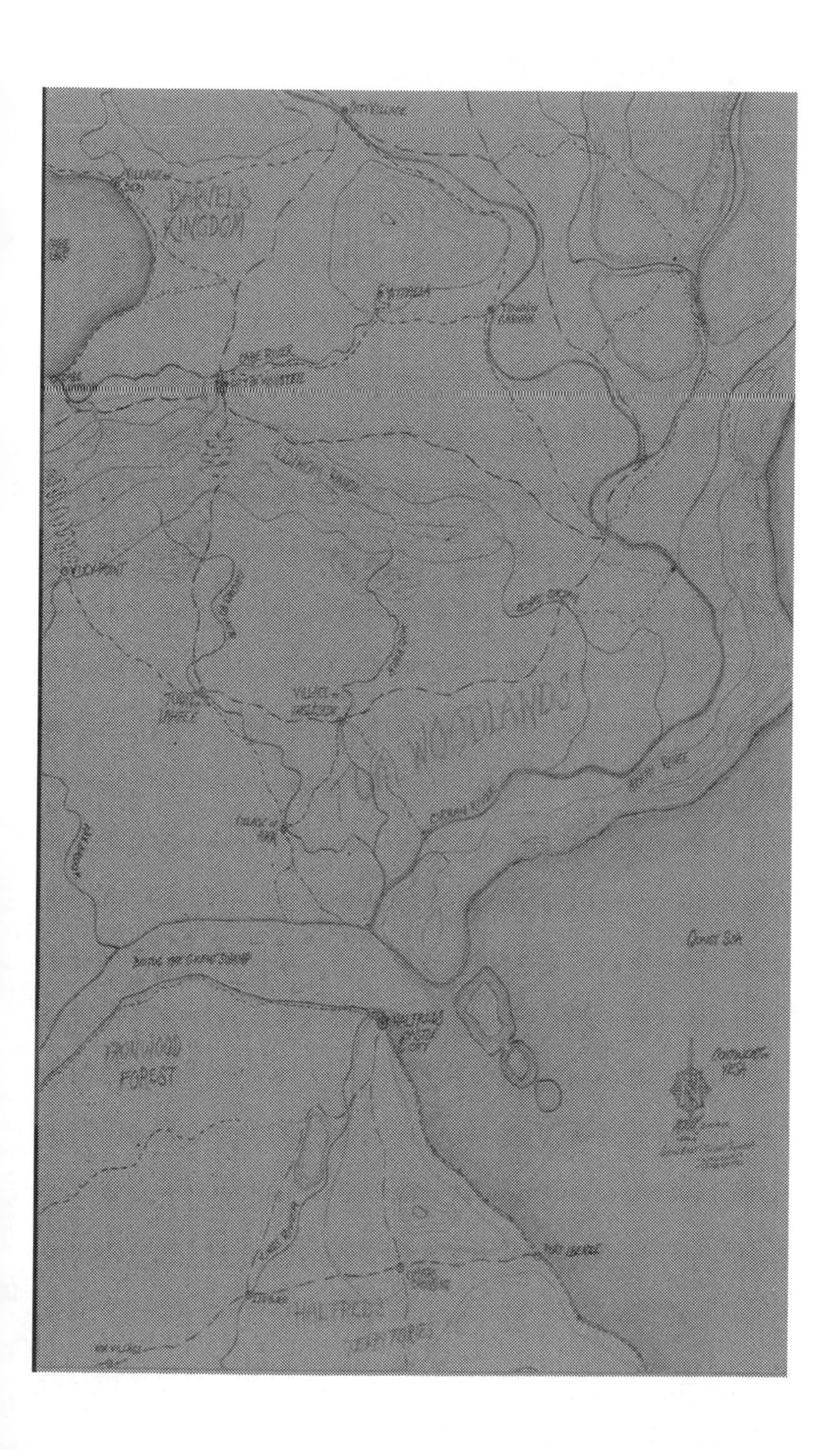
KINGDOM
WOODLANDS
FOREST

Chapter One
Setting Out

The last good days of summer are coming to an end. The rest of the farms' crops will need to be harvested soon. Followed by the long, dull winter months. Spent mostly keeping the old farmhouse warm. Still trying to make a name for himself, the skilled young rogue prepares for one more caper.

Inspecting each piece of his worn black dragon scale armor before strapping them in place Carr thinks. "A few more jobs… or perhaps this one and I can retire this fine old suit. It's survived a few generations…and the last three years, I've put it through hell."

Finishing with the shin coverings Carr takes a last check of the items in his backpack. One dirty cloak, two weeks of rations, some bandages wrapped around some healing herbs. The family lock picks, just as old as the scale armor and a small leather sack.

Making some room he adds a grappling hook and new coil of hemp rope.

"I hope this one holds up better than the last." He mumbles, briefly rubbing his right shoulder.

Then slips the pack and his favorite custom, sheathed long-sword on his back.

From the table he gathers two well balanced throwing daggers, sliding them into sheaths, hidden in his body armor.

Grabbing the handle of the exterior door Carr pauses looking back at a large roof support post. Hanging from it a bow and its quiver; holding only six arrows. Nodding to himself he decides to take them.

Outside he calls to a tan mix breed horse pacing already saddled in the front pen of the ageing barn. "Well Bressi girl. Are you ready for a bita rid'n?"

Seeming to understand Bressi nods her head.

"That's good…" Smiling, Carr opens the pen gate. "…cause' this may be the last time you'll get to run, this year."

He checks the straps of the horse's tack before leading Bressi from the corral.

Closing and securing the gate Carr easily hops up onto his saddle. Bressi knowing where to go eagerly starts trotting across the open property to the narrow trail that winds northeast through the surrounding Tau Woodlands.

Cool breezes find their way through the forest canopy blowing across the pair as they reach a wide but seldom used path.

"I hope it doesn't rain." Wondering he looks up sniffing the air. Fluffy white clouds swiftly float south.

Shrugging they follow the path north.

Something off to the left seems to catch Bressi's eye. In tune with her, Carr cautiously scans the brush. A chill rolls over him as if being stared at.

A couple weeds move next to them Carr's heart-rate increases his hand slowly reaches back for the hilt of his sword. Bressi remains calm and watchful.

Following her line of sight Carr spots a quick flash of fur. "A small critter." He whispers. Knowing even the tiniest of beasties, can have teeth, claws and attitude, he grips the sword.

Jumping quickly to the next patch of weeds reveals a rough tri-coloured cat missing a piece of its right ear and most of its tail.

"Shoulda guessed." Carr sighs with relief. "Damn Cat." Letting go of the sword, uttering. "Curious? Or are you, going to actually try and follow us all the way?" Staring at the farm cat as it crouches, trying to stay in the shadows.

Annoyed that he's been spotted the cat pretends not to be interested in Carr and Bressi, faking a little grooming, giving up its pursuit.

Carr chuckles at the cat. "Whatever cat." Thinking about the first time the cat had come around. At least four years, wintering in the barn, the rest of the year wandering the woods. Never has Carr managed to get close enough to touch it.

After a couple hours the tree line begins to break, ahead the small, quiet farming village of Ahn. A place Carr has spent much time and the townsfolk know.

Most don't trust him and the others have mixed opinions. Since he's never been caught stealing in Ahn, the people let him be.

Thin puffs of smoke rise from most of the small buildings. Carried with it the smells of assorted foods being cooked.

A group of dirty barefooted children play fighting draw his attention. Two boys toss each other about; the youngest barely able to run; try imitating them. Getting the other kids laughing at their pitiful attempts, Carr chuckles as well.

The girls notice Carr nearing and get quiet. A chubby ten year old sees what the girls do and pokes the arm of the boy next to him. A long black, haired boy looks up, still snickering at the little ones.

"Hey!" the boy exclaims with a smile "Hey, Carr!" poking his chubby friend back. " Its' just Carr." He leaves the group to meet Carr as he enters Ahn.

Carr waves slightly, hiding a smile knowing well the nine year old boy. Also knowing he's going to be used, to show off to the other children. Carr will certainly play along.

The older boys follow one by one, the girls dare not, instead keep the young ones back.

"Where are you off to?" The boy asks.

Carr slows Bressis' pace to respond. "A kindly old lady was forced to hand over two magical rings. To an evil greedy man saying it's payment to King Darvel, In order to gain his protection. Bah! I say to that crap."

The boys stay back a pace or two, one asks. "Who's King Darvel?"

The older boys make fun of his ignorance, the long dark haired boy turns back to answer him. "Don't you remember the other week that fancy carriage with those thirty armored horsemen came through. They were collecting anything valuables for King Darvel?" Seeing the other boy is still thinking about it. "Geez, did you just move here? My Pa's been complaining about him ever since. We'd never paid taxes before. Why now?"

"What are taxes?" Responds the dim boy.

Sighs and shaking heads are given from the boys.

"Your Pa's right Effim." Carr states, "The towns around here were settled long, long ago outside of any Kings Territory." Sitting tall he boasts. "That's why I must retrieve those magical rings before they become lost in the King's treasure vaults."

"Yah, well…" Effim hesitates remembering something he'd like. "Hey, can you ah, get me… That collectors' short sword?"

Carr ponders the request while digging in his body armor, for a coin pouch; listening to the boys talk.

"Who is that? Anyways?"

"That's Carr."

"My Pa says he's a thief."

"My Ma says he's trouble."

"Well my sister thinks he's cute"

"Your sister thinks ogres are cute."

"Hah, my Pop told me he was raised by rats."

Carr tries not to laugh pulling out the pouch speaking to Effim. "Has your Pa, any of his fine arrows to sell?"

"Not yet." Effim watches Carr dipping into the coin pouch. "That tax collector and his butt-weasels took everything he had and a couple of bows too."

"Hmm, that's no good." Carr wonders what the boy's father is going to do the next time the collector comes around.

Effim informs him. "He's been out every day gathering stuff to make new ones."

"Good." Carr tosses the boy a silver and gold coin. "The silver's for you"

Effim snaps the coins from the air before they have time to reflect in the sunlight. "Thanks!"

Carr tells him. "The gold is for your father. Tell him, I would like a dozen of his finest. I should be back by the next full moon."

Effim examines the coins as the boys gather around. "Sure I'll tell him…How's your shoulder? Did you get a new rope?"

A little embarrassed Carr replies. "Yah, I did." Continuing on, he waves. "See you when I get back."

More interested in showing off to the boys Effim stops outside his round mud hut. Without looking at Carr, he waves back. " See yah, good luck, and don't forget to bring me the collector's short sword."

Chuckling to himself, "Kids can be a great source of information." Carr nudges Bressi to pick up the pace, "I wonder which sister thinks I'm cute. I hope it's not that Doris."

Passing Sonja's home he sees only her mother and younger brother are inside. Carr sighs under his breath thinking about Sonja's pretty face with her long blonde hair blowing freely in the wind.

Taking the northern road out of Ahn, he barely takes notice of the men working the fields.

From the woods ahead the sounds of giggling girls can be heard, he hopes for a much better sight.

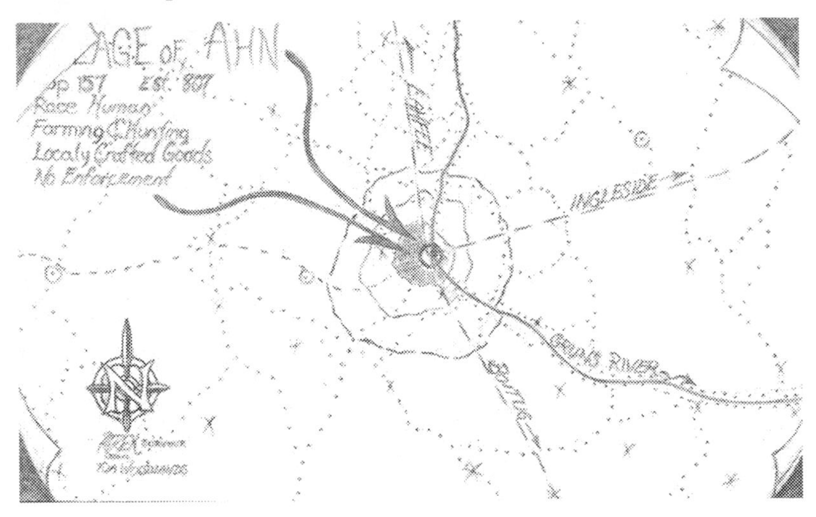

Sure enough rounding the lightly wooded road, Sonja, hair tied in a ponytail, her developing body is filling out her long pale yellow dress. If only she wasn't accompanied by her best friend

Doris, a rough girl of seven to eight stone in weight. Of course tagging along Doris' little and trying sister.

"Yoo, Hoo Carr!" Doris calls out, "Where are you off to? This time?"

Carr thinks, "Oh God, do I stop or go on?" Still happy to see Sonja he responds with a smile, "Hello, ladies. It's a nice day and I' d love to stay and chat," glancing at Sonja, "but I've a long way to travel before dusk." Getting closer. "By the wonderful smells from the village, I'd say your suppers, will be ready soon."

"Oh," Sonja simply says smiling up at Carr, "Thanks for telling us, we were just saying how hungry we're getting."

"Hi, Carr." Says Doris' sister "We were going to run off to Lahfee, to see the Minstrels."

Doris nudges her sister to be quiet, "It's too far to walk and I could eat a whole chicken right now."

Carr can't help but stare at Sonja "I'm headed there but we'd need a cart to all go and I don't think your parents would be very pleased about yous traveling with me."

"Ahh," Doris likes the idea. "You'd really take us?" Trying to encourage the others. "We can take my dad's cart, we'll be back by morning."

Carr informs her, "By tomorrow morn, we'd finally reach Lahfee."

"Dad would kill all of us." Exclaims Doris' sister.

Sonja uncomfortable by the idea, "Mine too. Maybe another year older they'd let us go."

"Maybe." Grinning at Carr, Doris remarks, "Maybe if we were escorted."

Carr is sure that'll never happen, "I doubt they'll ever let you ladies travel with me," winking at Sonja, "but it doesn't mean that I wouldn't mind."

Slightly jealous of the attention Sonja's been getting lately, Doris comments. "Ooo, Carr wants to take you away, Sonja." Nudging her slightly in jest, "I won't tell your parents. Right away."

"Funny, Doris." Sonja says not amused, "Well we best be off." Turning to Carr, "Have a safe journey."

"Yah, Sure." Carr replies. "You look out for each other." Waving goodbye, he and Bressi keep moving.

"I do." States Doris waving

Her sister belts out "Goodbye! Ratboy!" As the girls continue giggling their way home.

Glancing back to watch Sonja as long as possible Carr grumbles to himself. "Why couldn't I have been stuck with a better nick-name than Carr… I thank you scholar for teaching me to speak right and read in different languages…but to be known as a rat in orc and alike tongue. It's an insult in most lands…I, I could just curse him." Sighing, as Sonja's obscured by the trees, he turns to the road ahead.

"Ah, well. It's like Pa said, best if no one knows your real name." Nudging Bressi to move quicker. "And I do like some of the stories told about me."

Recounting the stories to Bressi, the sun slowly sets bringing them to a familiar spot to camp for the night. A small clearing surrounded by large trees and two boulders for cover.

Tying Bressi close to some edible vegetation, Carr surveys the area. Noticing his woodpile has been strewn about and a few long broken sticks.

The soft dirt ground is covered in small foot and boot prints. Figuring it most of been some of the village kids, out farther than they should be. The sticks were likely pretend swords.

With a small fire started and the forest dark; Carr nibbles on his rations while fashioning two cheaply crafted wooden swords, before nodding off.

Refreshed for the new day Carr makes sure to leave the wooden swords leaning against a boulder, to be seen by whom ever enters the area first.

Only the sparse sightings of the woodlands tamer critters, helped pass the day away. Except for the grey skies and having to fend off the occasional biting fly, the trek through Tau today was pleasant.

Reaching the almost barren landscape of Lahfee, a thriving small town of four hundred twenty three. More when the wanders and nomadic tribes hold up for the winter here.

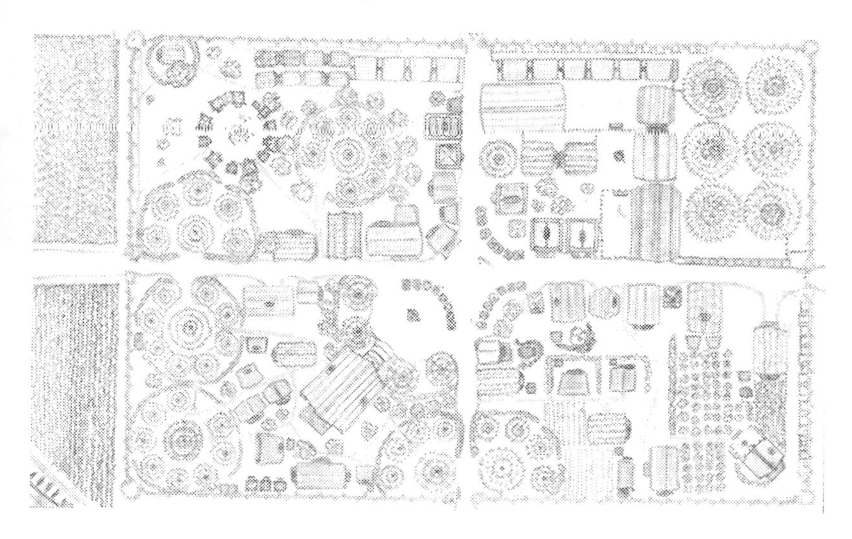

Settled in the seventh century by goblins, many of their huts still exist. Two centuries later other races started settling in.

Now mainly human and goblin with many common foe, they cleared the once surrounding woods. Erecting a simple fortified wall encircling the entire town. The land closest to the town was turned into good farmland.

In the thirty years the walls had been there no battle has been fought. It has saved them from rampaging beasts and prevented the buildings from being washed away in a mysterious flood two years ago. To Carr, this is the last chance for a warm meal before crossing the Ildihom mountain range.

Crossing a rickety wooden bridge to the south gate of Lahfee, Carr watches a few of the town's youths, wading in Gruns River giving spear-fishing a go. It looks more like horseplay, taking little notice of him.

Looking to the gates for today's voluntary guards sit two over aged males, curiously checking over him.

One goblin very pale almost human in colour. The other is a stout human. Both look very comfortable and set in their ways. They sit upon upright pieces of logs, with spears leaning out of reach on the wall, sharing a pipe.

Smoking something familiar, Carr has no time for that, with a job at hand.

"Greetings young man." The stout sentry says, curious to how he replies. "What brings you to Lahfee?" Pointing up. "Shelter from the storm?"

Carr doesn't look but responds with a smile. "Good day men, I hadn't decided whether to stay the night. Just a last good meal before taking on the pass and its lurking beasties."

Appreciating the friendly and basic information the old men seem content with Carr's character. The men barely move only to pass their pipe.

In his own mumbling tongue the goblin feels out Carr. "A good meal here? Better to eat bugs."

Carr doesn't completely understand him but responds. "Might as well eat bugs, Eh?"

The stout man chokes on his smoke filled lungs surprised that Carr understood the old slurring goblin's speech.

Content the young human understands, the goblin continues. "Testing you. Eat at the old tavern. The cart merchants are selling the remains of weak animals killed by others."

Carr stops briefly beside the two men trying to figure out what the old goblin just said.

Spitting out a glob of brownish flem the stout man clears his throat. "Eat at the…" coughing a few more times, "Whew… couldn't catch my breath."

Carr doesn't look surprised by his statement. "Please don't die on me. I'd most likely get blamed because I'm not from here."

Both men chuckle at the sad truth.

The stout one finishes what he was trying to say. "Yah, anyway, just eat at the old tavern. At the center of town. The food's at least edible. There's a couple huts you could rent for the night. Unfortunately you missed the minstrels…"

"For a bunch of gangly humans. They were okay." Interrupts the goblin speaking human.

Thinking about Sonja and Doris, Carr mentions. "Minstrels are gone, eh? While passing through Ahn, a couple young, pretty ladies wanted me to escort them here, to hear them play."

Curious about new females the old men lean forward. "How young.?"

Carr answers. "Ah, year or two, younger than I."

The old men lean back waving their hand dismissively, the human mutters "Old enough to breed, no damn fun though."

Agreeing the goblin nods adding. "They never show their true form until popping out a few pups."

With a grin and shaking his head at his buddy, the human says. "Yah the Minstrels left, the day after the Tax collector's party rolled through. Taken joyous times with them."

"Hmmf" The goblin grumbles.

Trying not to sound too suspicious Carr inquires. "Is the tax collector headed back to Monsteil?"

The old guys see a purpose in the young rogue's journey, glancing briefly at one another with a knowing eye. With no care for the Darvel name the goblin leans in looking cautiously about for spies.

Speaking clearly to Carr, the goblin informs him. "Today he should have left Vixy point back to Monsteil by the morning of the third day."

His human buddy looks amazed by what he told.

Carr knows information like that is always worth rewarding, reaching for his coin pouch. "Is that so? Darvel is stretching his reach all the way around."

The goblin answers, "Yah, and I don't want your coin." pointing towards Monsteil. "I wanna live long enough to hear someone got those pale greedy, gutless windbags. Somehow, someday," turning to his buddy, "and I still like to hear about what happens to those who fail trying."

The old man nods puffing away, motioning to Carr to keep his eyes and ears open.

Not sure what to think of them Carr politely moves on. "Well, gentlemen thank you for sharing such information." Sounding confident. "You'll get to hear one of those stories. How much of it will be true?"

The human asks, "Young sir, tell us your name. So we'll know who to listen for."

Carr answers in orc, " Ratboy of the swamp clan." A title, local kids call him. Speaking in human. "But most just call me Carr."

With raised brows the old men look at each other, and smile at the strange choice in title. The human shrugs; figuring this will be the first and last time they will see the young male. "Good-luck, young man." They utter shaking their heads at the foolish pursuits of the young.

Entering the town most people are preoccupied with their own lives. As many mercenaries regularly pass through, Carr's armor doesn't stand out, badly.

Making his way to the center of town he ponders better titles. "Could be Prince Carr, ha hardly, Sir Carr of Boitug. Nah…the Great Swamp Rat."

Spotting the old tavern he ties Bressi up beside several other horses. Looking at the sagging roof of the building, Carr decides to sit at a table not sheltered by the roof.

Immediately a middle-aged goblin woman greets him pleasantly. "Good evening; a drink or perhaps something to eat?"

Looking into the woman's eyes with a smile, Carr compliments her. "Hello; if I was a little more mature I'd ask for something other then a bowl of hot stew and a mug of mead." Carr winks at her.

Liking how the young human responds to her, she lightly touches his jaw. "I've got a great venison stew your gonna enjoy" She winks. "I'll be back."

"Okay." Carr replies thinking. "Try that stuff on any human woman they're offended or think you're up to something. Races like orcs, goblins and such aren't known for having great romantic lovers. No matter the race, women seem to have strange romantic ideas and even if your not what they want, they like to know you want them...Wait what about Carr the Swooner, Thief of Hearts."

The barmaid returns to see him staring blankly. "Hey, your not going to pass out on me, are yah?" Setting down a large wooden bowl of hot thick stew."You look like you need it." She sets the mead down and gets a wooden spoon from her apron.

"Oh thank you.'" Carr smells it and smiles at her. "This is going to hit the spot."

Handing him the spoon. "Tell me how it is?"

Being no surprises in goblin cooking, Carr digs out a large spoonful, and shovels it into his mouth. A bit warm but quite bland, as gesture of goblins and orcs is to grunt their opinions with mouths full, if its truly good they just keep eating. Carr spits out. "Tasty."

Content with the reply the women smiles. "Very good. Get it into yah. You could use to put on another stone." Patting his shoulder she carries on.

Half way through the bowl Carr's belly fills, sitting back to finish his mead a single raindrop splashes on his hand. Looking up to dark skies closing from the northeast. "Better keep moving." Wishing to avoid heavy rain and hoping to catch the tax collector, before what's been collected ends up in the treasury vaults of Monsteil Castle.

Reaching for some coins he asks the nearing goblin barmaid. "Kind lady, what do I owe?"

She steps right over to him, "Four silver," noticing he's only eaten half, "Is there something wrong with the stew?"

Assuring her Carr replies. "No just too much for my little belly." Pointing to the sky. "I'd like to keep moving before the rains start."

Looking up she notices a lightning flash. "That doesn't look like just a little rain. You should just hold up in town for the night." Grinning slyly. "I've got a hut you could rent for the night. For a young cutie like you I'd let yah, get away with just another silver."

Wondering about her intent, Carr responds smiling. "A single gold to be bed and fed an excellent deal." Placing a gold coin on the table. "Your offer is one I have to turn down."

"Why's that?" She inquires disappointed.

"I need to reach Monsteil in three days." Still smiling Carr slides the coin to her. "Keep it all and remember me, I should be back in a week. I'll be looking for another good meal and a dry bed."

The smile returns as she quickly places the coin in the pouch, clinking with several others. "Anytime you come through, stop in and I'll take care of you."

"Very good then," Carr stands bowing slightly to her, "Thank you kind woman. I'll be certain to see you the next time through." Leaving to untie Bressi.

"Safe journey young man." She watches him leave while cleaning up.

Quickly leaving Lahfee Carr easily coaxes Bressi to a gallop. Following the northern road between the fields, passing farm workers headed home.

After crossing a sturdier bridge over the Gruns

river they reach the cover of the woods as the sky blackens and the rains start.

An hour of trotting up the winding road the storm catches them, strong winds bat around the trees allowing the heavy rainfall to penetrate.

Branches throughout can be heard cracking and snapping off their trees, then crash down.

Flashes of lightning periodically illuminate the road; Creating eerie, moving shadows, followed by claps of thunder, keeping Carr's mind alert and Bressi on edge.

Becoming wet Carr talks attempting to calm Bressi and himself. "So-kay girl it's just a lot of noise, we'll be just fine."

"Crack! Crack! Crack!" a large nearby branch breaks away tearing through the other trees as it goes down, startling Carr and Bressi.

"Easy girl. Easy." Carr pulls back on the reins keeping Bressi from bolting. "We're gonna be okay, I hope. Out here at this time there are so many other things to be concerned about; Wild hungry beasts, savage parties of wanderers, lurking thieves and cutthroats. Never thought I'd be taken out b..."

The surrounding area lights up briefly as a bolt of lightning shoots out, it forks, splitting an old tree they just passed. The immediate booming thunder sends Bressi racing; before the tree splits; they're gone.

Carr tries to stay in the saddle, bouncing about. Jerking on the reins has no affect, Bressi is taking her own course, leaving the road and tearing into the woods. Staying low he grips the saddle tight waiting for Bressi to slow or stop.

Branches, twigs and vines whip across them. With every loud crash and boom Bressi changes her direction. Carr has no idea where they are, how long she's been running or when she'll stop, as his eyes are closed tight praying to stay on.

After one of the longest and wildest rides, Bressi stops and slowly turns herself around. Opening his eyes and loosening his now cramping hands, Carr sees his horse has found shelter, in a shallow but tall opening in a rock formation.

Sliding off the saddle he pats Bressi. "Alright I guess we can hold up here." His hands and face have many nicks, but nothing that needs attention.

Bressi turns her head away from him shaking it.

Seeing his horse isn't very happy he crouches by the opening watching the storm pass.

Soon the rains slow and the shivering starts, Carr scours the area looking for anything that'll still burn.

Managing to find enough semi-dry wood Carr gets a small fire started, close to the opening. He sits down to dry and ease the shivers.

The rains stop and clouds break, by midnight, still not dry the chills pass and Carr begins to nod off.

"Snap," a stick breaks nearby, giving Carr's heart a jolt. He scans the dark woods, Bressi tries to sniff the air but the wind flows towards the noise.

Carefully easing his sword from its sheath, making only the slightest of sound. He glances back to see if Bressi detects anything.

"Crack." An old branch breaks. Bressi becomes agitated. Carr rises moving in front of the fire, allowing his eyes to adjust to the dark.

"Who's out there?" Carr utters firmly.

Bressi's ears perk up. She backs up in the shelter, making Carr nervous. The sounds of something two legged, is moving slowly towards them.

Carr yells in orc, "What do you want?" easily understood by most races.

A smell as foul as a hundred unwashed feet wafts in, Bressi snorts with disgust, Carr almost gags.

From the shadows steps a big figure, threatening in ogre. "Your shit. Your horse or your life."

Carr doesn't need to know what was exactly said, as his eyes widen studying the fifteen stone ogre, standing at least ten spans tall. Carrying what appears to be a small tree over his shoulder. Stepping closer to size up this young human.

Carr gulps thinking, "That's no tree, that's a spiked club as big as me." Taking a couple deep breaths in an attempt to stay calm.

Ogres only give up after victory, maiming or death and it isn't scared of Carr.

The ogre steps closer, Carr readies himself as they are almost in striking distance of each other.

The ogre takes another step, Carr rushes in with a hard wild swing. The ogre swings his club, Carr's sword grazes the ogre's midsection as they pass leaving a minor cut. The club connects with Carr's back, no spikes pierce him but the force sends him sailing into a large tree. Dislodging the long-sword from his grip.

On the ground and winded Carr feels for his blade.

The ogre quickly moves in, grabbing Carr by his long hair and flings him back. Carr's body connects hard with rock. Dazed and winded he shakily searches for his daggers.

Laughing manically, the ogre points the spiked club at Carr; speaking in ogre while moving closer. "Now you die little man."

Not hearing the ogre but seeing a double image of it raising the club overhead for a fatal blow. Carr pulls forth a dagger mustering his strength and focus, whipping the dagger towards the ogre's head, sadly aiming at the wrong head.

As the ogre starts to swing, Carr's thrown blade manages to strike the ogre's weapon hand. The blade tip dives into the ogre's thumb, momentarily pinning it to the club. The ogre's opposing force allows the dagger to sever the thumb. Following through the club escapes the wielder's grip, gauging Carr's left arm coverings as it slams down.

The ogre screams out in pain, Carr grabs a handful of dirt getting on his feet.

Turning pain to anger the ogre rushes. Carr lets the dirt fly blinding the ogre and avoids him.

Hoping to use the large club Carr bends over to pick it up, but its way too heavy for him. The ogre aggressively flails its arms about trying to connect with the young male. Instead stumbles into Carr.

Carr is knocked aside by his foe's sheer size, the ogre losses balance tripping on a big piece of rock, falling hard face first on the ground.

Seizing the opportunity Carr swiftly jumps on its' back, drawing out his last dagger driving the blade deep into the back of the ogre's neck; Twisting the blade Carr severs the ogre's brain stem.

Convulsing violently Carr is shaken off. He watches the body until it stops moving.

Kicking the ogre to make sure it's dead Carr leans over to pluck out his dagger. Wiping the blade off on the ogre's shirt Carr returns the dagger to its sheath.

Calming down he stumbles backwards accidentally kicking the rest of his collected wood into the fire.

Gesturing to himself, "Easy, relax." Sitting down near Bressi, Carr leans against the rock.

Taking a deep breath to finish calming, he watches the small flames dance about in the fire.

It's not long before Carr falls asleep.

Chirping birds wake Carr, opening an eye to smoldering ashes. Shaking his head to snap to, he notices the woods are beginning to lighten. Bressi is nearby eating.

Looking around stretching he sees the fallen foe. Curious if the ogre has anything of value he gets up with a big noisy yawn.

Checking out the ogre's fatal wound Carr pulls back its heavy hide shirt collar, spotting a gold chain.

Gagging on a foul stench that pours out he turns away as his eyes water from the vapors.

Releasing the collar, "Ah, blauck!... You stinky bastard!" Kicking its side, "You're barely dead."

Carr turns spiting frequently, as the stench lingers on his tongue.

Seeing an old Bay Berry tree Carr snags a leaf immediately chewing on it. "Better." Starring at the ogre shaking his head. "I can't believe that smell." Sighing, "I can't believe I'm gonna search this guy."

Taking in a deep breath Carr runs at the ogre, going in with momentum to roll the heavy body. He grabs its shoulder and sides lifting at the same time. He gets the body partially up putting his own shoulder and weight against the ogre's stiffening body. Digging in with his feet a big grunt and heave Carr manages to roll the male over with a thud.

Landing across the ogre's body, Carr pushes himself up forgetting not to breath, he inhales a lungful of the stench.

Now puking up the last of the venison stew Carr moves back getting some good air; another leaf and let things settle.

Bressi stops to watch him, most of the small woodland creatures flee the area or go into hiding.

Approaching Bressi for his canteen Carr spots his first dagger laying close to a bloody thumb.

Sheathing it Carr wonders looking around. "Now I just need to find my sword." Patting Bressi's hindquarters. "Have you seen it girl?"

The horse pokes him with her nose getting his attention and moves forward.

"Where are you going?" Carr quietly asks trying to retrieve the canteen from the saddlebag. Turning to look where she's going, he sees his sword laying in a patch of weeds. "Oh. Thanks

Bressi, you're a good girl." patting her neck as he moves in front of her. "Really smart, good girl. Yes you are."

Her head seems to nod yes like she already knew that, getting Carr to chuckle.

Having removed the sheath from his back Carr gasps. "Ohh, there's a crack in it." Following the crack he gasps again. "Ah, damn it there's a hole right through it." Certain it came from the blow to his back. "Well at least its still in one piece." Inserting the long-sword blade in, he shows it to Bressi. "Hey its Okay."

Disinterested Bressi goes back to nibbling, Carr slings the sword onto his back and goes for the canteen and a bit of rations.

Now feeling ready to check out the ogre, Carr sees the male has a rusty, sword in a matching sheath tied around his side. Tied to the sheath strap a small filthy pouch. It contains coins, opening it to find eleven copper coins. Not much but he adds them to his.

Carr Jests, "It'll at least pay for dinner" looking at his on the ground.

Stepping back for fresher air Carr uses his long sword to open the ogre's shirt to view his necklace.

Returning the blade Carr sees it's a long thick gold chain with a well crafted, platinum medallion hanging from it. Holding his breath he gets a closer look at it.

"A Medallion of Protection." Finding and opening the chain's clasp Carr pulls it from around the ogre's neck. Stepping back to check its markings closely, a smile slowly crosses his face.

Chuckling Carr uselessly points out to the dead male. "Stupid ogre, this is meant to protect those of good heart, it's a curse to evil souls like you." Looking at the medallion, "Better for me…"

Carr hesitates before trying it on. For the first time in a few years he wonders if all the stealing, lying, and killings have corrupted his soul.

Thinking of what respected elders have said and certain the Gods know he had good intentions taking on the jobs he did.

Shrugging it all off he tries it on, looking about with squinted eyes Carr waits to see if anything bad happens to him.

Pushed, Carr stumbles forward, "Hey!" Staying upright he turns to see its Bressi, nudging him. "Oh are you telling me its time to get going?"

Bressi nods once, getting Carr to laugh.

The sun has risen far enough to illuminate the area. The niche they stopped in, is part of a long rock shelf and the start of the Idlihom Mountain range.

Knowing only that the mountain pass is to the west Carr leads Bressi northwest. Making their way up the increasingly rocky terrain.

Mid morning Carr reaches a high cliff base leading up to one of the ranges highest peaks. Unfortunately he's too close, to see the top.

Following the base Carr happens across an animal trail winding up the mountainside.

Turning into the hardest part of his journey, the trail follows a section of the mountainside having the appearance it tried to separate, long ago.

After every rough section they carefully traverse the tree coverage lessens. Each level starts with an outlook point, close to tight groups of tall standing rock. Most stand taller than him and contain exposed crystalline veins of pale yellows and pinks.

Reaching the sixth and final level, the trail continues amongst thick brush and sparse trees.

Enjoying the view Carr takes a break.

Identifying an eastern peak he figures they've still a ways to go before finding the mountain pass. Looking back the way they came Carr marvels at natures' simple beauty. He can see each level of the standing rocks almost in a straight line. The noontime sunlight catches the occasional crystalline vein producing glittering flashes.

Towards the south he can barely make out the towns of Lahfee and Ingleside, they look only a stone's throw from each other. Ahn isn't visible to him but he knows where it is, south of that home.

Thinking to himself, "I wonder if Ma could see me up here?" he waves.

Seeing the blue green of the great swamp he follows it east to the ocean a deep blue covers everything past the coastal Akemi mountain range.

Ready to carry on Carr speaks to Bressi taking her rein. "Great path we found. Hope I can find it again."

The trail eventually comes to a fork, heading up east or down and west. Staying true to course they head west.

Carr thinks about stories told of an old green dragon that lives in this range and of course giants have been here for centuries. Though never seeing any such beings here before, Carr still constantly and carefully checks about.

Ahead the path turns around a rock formation. Carr's heightened senses make out a faint noise and Bressi wants to back up.

Cautious, he ties Bressi to a tree and stealthily scouts out the path ahead.

Nearing the bend, he hears the chilling sound of flesh being torn from bone and being eaten.

Locating the source, behind the rock formation. Driven by sheer curiosity Carr picks his movements and coverage getting closer to see what kind of beast is up here, with him.

"Crack! Snap!" A large bone breaks. Followed by an awful sucking sound.

Carr prays to himself, "Great Chislev beautiful guardian of the earth; please let this be one of your fury predators and not a dragon outside its den. Although I would like to find an unoccupied lair."

Holding up behind a tree trunk Carr can see something moving past a large pine tree; in a small area behind the formation, it's tan in colour. Sure it's a big cat dinning on something,

Carr still wants to get closer. Deciding to risk crossing the path, to the pine tree.

Quickly he darts across while the beast is tearing a piece of flesh off. The tree's branches hang too low to hide under quietly.

A span out to far, he sees there's brush on the other side of the tree obscuring the creature. Carr does manage to see the tail of a cat whip out briefly.

Certain it's a mountain lion and feeling exposed Carr decides to creep back. He hesitates seeing something flash by the corner of his eye.

Carr thinks a second, "Was that a really big wing?" Taking a second look he can't see properly. "It's a big cat eating a big bird, but bird bones don't break like the one I heard."

Looking at the rock formation just a long jump away, Carr dares himself to make a foolish dash.

As the beast digs in and begins to remove more flesh, Carr dashes to the rocks catching a glimpse of something he needs to process first.

Back against the wall and out of sight he replays the sighting in his head a giant mountain lion, with a huge black and grey mane and a big pair of folded feathered wings.

Unknown to Carr the breeze he created dashing past was enough to alert the creature. It silently leaps atop the formation over Carr, sitting curiously watching the young human.

Now worried Carr thinks, "What the hell was that?" The colour starts to leave his face. "A manticore.?! I'm done for. No it can't be?"

Hoping he has not just encountered one of the wilds' fabled, evil creatures, he cautiously peeks around the corner. Stretching farther out Carr quickly realizes it's not there anymore. Only a partially eaten mountain goat sprawled across a large flat rock. Blood from the animal is all over.

Putting his back to the formation, Carr feels like being stared through. Scanning the area around, he realizes the creature is probably above, Carr's hand slowly moves for his sword hilt.

Stopping Carr, the creature sternly growls using an old human language. "Do it and die."

A language not used anymore, but was taught to Carr in case he should happen across ancient books or scrolls. Today those lessons are going to aid him.

Understanding what was said, he extends his fingers, distancing his hand from sword slowly turning. Looking up the formation, Carr puts a face to a fable.

Sitting comfortable, out of easy striking distance; a winged lion, as big as a draft horse, with the head of male being; A very big head with bushy graying black hair. Its' long beard and mustache are soaked with blood and patches of goat fur. It can hear Carr's heart rate increase and smell a faint bit of fear coming off his body.

Feeling Carr is no real threat the creature asks. "Up here, alone, why?"

Thanking Chislev for this being a creature of some intelligence, Carr replies shakily. "Crossing over for Monsteil city." Not sure he's spoken the right words.

The creature understands and believes him but the armor and young age make him wonder what he's up too. "Dark, dragon scale armor, why?" pointing with a bloody black claw tipped paw. "Soft boots, Monsteil city, why?"

Surprised by the beings' observation, Carr wonders how to respond, taking a second. "I cause you worry?"

Much like a cat he starts cleaning his face. "Yes."

Carr wonder's why a monster sized beast would worry about him. "I want thing from Monsteil. Go home remove crops."

Thinking about what was said and not seeing Carr as a farmer, the creature cocks his head cutting to the chase. "You thief, Yes. Hhmm?"

Beads of sweat form, Carr fears answering him. "Ah, um, in some eyes."

Noticeable unhappy with the reply, the creature stares into Carr's soul. "Tell me what you seek."

Feeling faint Carr squeaks out, "Two, rings."

The answer honest, the creature wonders if he still has to worry about Carr, simply and calmly asking. "Explain? Please."

Still hoping to get out of this alive, Carr speaks slowly in an attempt to plead his case to gain safe passage. "King Darvel, sent men south, demanding, coin from people, for protection from his men."

The creature knows about tributes paid to leaders and if you don't you could be beaten, robbed, killed or jailed. Finding the jailed the most distasteful. He motions with his paw to continue.

"Ah, alright," Carr's pulse slows some as he goes on. "They found my farm, only my mother there…"

"They hurt your mother, you want revenge?" The creature interrupts.

"No." Carr tells him. " Mother said there was no money, they, knocked stuff over, looking for stuff, finding two nice swords and two rings. Swords, ah." Carr shrugs. "Rings important. I must retrieve."

Taking in Carr's story the creature sees his quest as believable and foolhardy. "You two legged creatures always risking life for things. My concern, men killing for fun or treasure."

Carr automatically thinks there's treasure nearby, but is more concerned with walking away for now. "Oh, I do not seek your treasure. I thought manticores just stories."

Offended the beast stands stretching out his great spanning wings darkening Carr, while roaring out "No manticore!"

Carr's mouth drops figuring he's just pissed off something more dangerous, speculating the odds of at least fending it off. "Sorry, I do not know, sorry."

Seeing Carr scared, the creature sits calmly stating. "I lammasu." Pointing to his puffed out chest.

Close to collapse, Carr exhales deeply. "lam,ma,su got it." Not sure he can take any more, he needs to know the unseen future. "You, play before killing?"

"I kill to eat and protect home." Laying on the rocks to finish cleaning up. "You worry me not." pointing towards Monsteil. "You die there I think."

Insulted but glad to know he's not going to get torn to pieces, Carr asks. "You let me go?"

"You make promise?" The lammasu asks.

Seeing the light at the end of the cavern, Carr eagerly answers. "Yes."

The creature firmly states. "Never speak of me, never look for me. Leave this area soon."

"Yes, I do promise, to just that." Carr stands stretching out his hand to seal the promise.

Strangely the lammasu stretches its' face out sniffing Carr's hand, sitting back he says. "I know where you live." Pointing directly towards the unseen farmhouse. "If I smell you, around here, after today. Or feel you did wrong to me. I will find and kill you." Saying it but not meaning it, "I do not find you. I find your mother."

"You do not need to do such things." Carr sighs once more. "The mountain road is west?"

The lammasu shakes his head at the idea of a young male lost in the mountains. "Yes stay west, east no good for you."

"Oh, thank you kind being." Carr has to ask. "Why east no good."

The lammasu stands stretching out body and wings simply saying, "Giants."

Carr questions whispering, "Giants?"

"Yes, giants." The creature replies, joking at his age and small size. "They take you home as play thing for children."

Carr doesn't like that idea, or the idea of being fought over by two giant kids and losing a limb.

The lammasu, disinterested in Carr, leaps high into air flapping its huge wings, blowing Carr's hair back.

Flying up the mountainside the lammasu vanishes from sight cresting the summit.

In awe of the experience Carr stands reflecting, before returning to Bressi.

After that the afternoon slipped by pleasantly as their new found trail eventually leads them to the main mountain pass.

Reaching the highest point by early evening, Carr takes a last look south, waving to his mother at home. A silly gesture, his father made years ago on their first trip over the range.

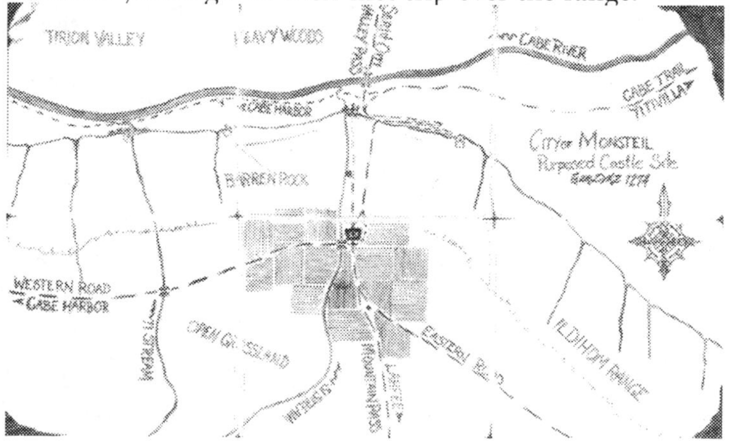

Turning north and starting to descend, he looks past the Tirion valley. To the row of independent mountains to the far northeast the last peak barely peeks over the curved horizon.

A Ship on Cabe lake sailing to the village of Seri, looks like a speck on the calm water's surface, it's white wake seems a mere ripple.

Glancing down to the mountain range's cliff base the city of Monsteil is almost recognizable. The Castle Monsteil north of the city seems like a boulder perched dangerously close to the cliff edge.

Too high to really tell but no one seems to be traveling on the roads.

Barely finding a well used camp-sight as the mountainside darkens; Carr stops for the night not lighting any fire, as not to draw attention.

Tonight he sits upon a rock gnawing on rations and enjoying the view.

The city slowly begins lighting torches individual flames can't be seen by Carr. After awhile the enclosed city glows like a distant candle.

Extending his arm and hand flat out. Pretending to hold the now tiny city of Monsteil in the palm of his hand. Carr threatens to drop them down the mountainside if they don't return the rings to him.

Laughing at himself he thinks of the story, of how the great stonewalls of Monsteil came to be.

After the walls were completed Carr's father; just a small boy at the time; was taken to the city, by his father. Telling him each time they went; how the walls were built. Carr has only heard the story a few times.

During his grandfather's days, the Darvel family was at war with northern orc and hobgoblin clans. Trying to take over the region all the way down to the Great Swamp.

The Idlihom clan of giants didn't want that to happen but were not yet a target. Choosing to sit up in the mountains much like where Carr is; watching repeated attacks on the once open city.

A castle once stood there it was said to have survived twenty sieges during its life.

The surrounding Kingdoms lost too many men and couldn't risk leaving their territories open to attack.

The orc's received aid from a few bored clans southwest of the Great Swamp. The orcs encountered the giants on the mountain range and tried to force their hand into choosing a side.

The giants not wishing to join them started a battle with the southern clans. Destroying half the southern clans, the surviving orcs did make it past. Joining up with the northern clans readying for a large scale, assault on Monsteil.

After having lost many good people the giants received a request from King Darvel's father, hoping they'd help fend off the next assault. The giants weren't interested in losing any more people.

They were informed if the orcs could fell Monsteil, the orc, hobgoblin and goblin clan leaders, of the rest of the northern continent, would commit their warriors to spread out destroying anything not with them; until the northern continent could be taken.

Unsure of the truth the giants said they would have to think it over. The King returned unhappy to his castle, figuring it's just him and his worn army. He sent all unable to fight down the eastern road to make a weeklong trek to King Halford's City, south of the Great Swamp.

Days later the clans came from two directions the west and north. As Darvel readied his army the giants decided to help. The older giants too slow to fight knocked stone piles free from the mountainsides. The women and older kids would toss the heavy stones and small boulders closer to Monsteil and awaiting able bodied giants.

The strange distraction unnerved the advancing clans. King Darvel and his men cheered and chanting excited to have the giant's aid.

That afternoon hundreds of orcs and hobgoblins were crushed to death. The clans in the valley never made it up the cliffs. Most fled complaining Darvel wasn't fighting fair. That humorous piece of information caused Darvel and the giants to try and help one another.

As a gesture of good will the giants picked up all the rocks and began building the walls. A pack of dwarf stonecutters cut the rocks to fit, the giants would place them.

With the walls progressing smoothly the dwarves challenged the giants to build the tallest and strongest wall seen by any creature with eyes. The giants actually enjoying the project were easily coaxed. Darvel certainly wasn't going to stop them. By the next fall they had completed they wall.

A grand ceremony was held people of neighboring tribes, towns and Kingdoms showed up. All leaders were impressed by the effort put out by three different races, who'd logically could never see eye to eye.

As the celebration dragged into the early morning, a few of the giants, not experienced drinkers, began drunkenly wrestling with each other. One giant tossed another, crashing him into the old Monsteil castle destroying a tall spire.

King Darvel's men also intoxicated tried to stop the giants from wrestling inside the city walls. As alcohol clouds the mind the situation took a turn for the worst.

Feeling as they weren't welcome in the city, the giants became agitated and demolished the castle.

A foolish battle started between the giants and Darvel's conscious men. A needless bloody fight lasting until the sun went down.

Its' citizens and visitors fled in fear of being crushed. Monsteil city was in ruins and the King and giants lost many people.

The new walls were barely damaged, but it took months to rebuild the most of the dwellings, and three years to build the new castle, that now sits on the edge of the cliffside.

The giants returned to the mountain range never to involve themselves in the affairs of others again.

Old King Darvel realized alcohol was the demise of their alliance and never pursued the giants, despite the requests of widows and merchants.

Chapter Two
The Job

The next morning Carr sets out early, knowing it's going to take the better part of the day to descend the mountain pass.

More then halfway down Carr notices a line of horsemen escorting a carriage on the west road, headed for the city.

"There's that bastard tax collector." Says Carr, pointing them out to Bressi. Happy to know the collections haven't been taken to the castle vaults.

He was hoping just to sneak into the their camp while they slept, to steal back the rings. Now he must try another plan. Break into the stone community affairs building in the city. Find where collections are stored or to be distributed, retrieve the rings and get out undetected. Better then attempting to sneak through the castle.

As Bressi carries on downward he pulls out a map of the city. Locating the building he runs plans and scenarios over in his head.

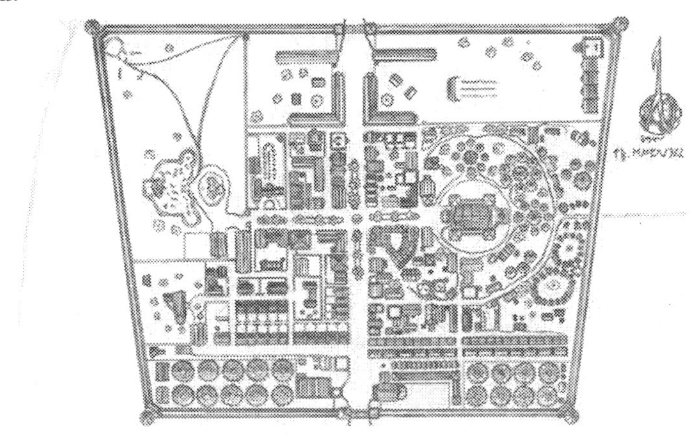

It's late afternoon by the time they reach the bottom, and over an hour still to travel before they reach Monsteil. Carr has several plans that require study of the actual surroundings of the building.

Lightly nudging Bressi's sides with his heels she picks up her pace.

A slight breeze from the north pushes in graying clouds slowly covering the skies above. The corner watchtowers along the tall, dark grey stonewalls begin to define themselves.

Carr slows Bressi as not to alarm the tower guards.

Passing between, the city's grain fields, Carr notices how thick and hardy they are. Impressed that soil, only a couple hands deep can produce such a nice crop and after all the decades of farming.

He then gives his head a shake, annoyed at himself for thinking about farming.

Deceiving to the eye the flat land and semi straight road makes the city seem close. Carr would love to get Bressi racing there but he'd be a target for a barrage of arrows. Or at least have the gates closed on him. With a deep exhale he keeps glancing ahead to see if the city walls appear any bigger.

The city's guards are aware of his approach.

Men from the fields make their way back to the city filling the road ahead. Carr tries to count the number of men but can't see them all. Getting to seventy-five he's content to say there are more than a hundred men tending the crops.

If he could have all their help, his fields would be cleared and stowed in a couple hours. Sighing, at the thought of it going to take him a couple weeks, sun up to sun down.

Catching up to the tail end of the workers as they file through the main gates, Carr notices all the guard's eyes are on him. Two males tending the entrance seem to want to exchange a few words with him.

Carr stops Bressi just as one of the men calls out "Halt! And state your business."

A normal question Carr was ready for. "I just wish a place for my horse and I to rest for the night. I'll be leaving at first light."

Humorously testing Carr's reaction, the older of the guards points to the creek just west of the city. "There you go. Should suit the likes of you just fine."

Surrounding men chuckle.

Also finding him humorous Carr replies. "It does but there's no mead or maiden." Also getting a couple laughs from the men.

"Alright." The guard grins. "I'll let you pass." In a stern voice he warns. "We catch you stealing. We'll find a place for you to rest." Then steps aside.

"I understand." Is all Carr dare say, keeping a friendly smile he gets Bressi moving.

The guards watch him, guessing with each other over what Carr is and up to.

Stopping at the public stables and dismounting Carr notices that most of the guards inside the city are checking him over.

An awkward young male exits the stable to take Bressi's reins.

Retrieving a silver coin Carr hands it to the stable-boy. "This is Bressi, she'll definitely need some water and grain."

"Thank-you sir." The stable-boy replies, pocketing the coin. "She's a pretty one, I'll take good care of her. When will you be leaving?"

Removing his bow and quiver from the saddle Carr answers. "As soon as the city gates open."

"Oh." The male points out "You're lucky."

Carr asks. "Why's that?"

The male smiles showing horse like teeth. "I'm here before that. I'll make sure to have her ready."

"That would be great if you could." Carr smiles.

"Are you headed for the battle in the Qulun Territories?" Inquires the stable-boy leading Bressi to a water trough.

Not knowing anything about it Carr answers. "Yes." Before the male can ask anything else he turns to leave. "Thanks again and I'll see you two in the morning. Good night."

Watching Carr walk away the stable-boy utters, "See you then." while petting Bressi.

Passing the row-housing built for field workers, Carr checks to see what shops are still on the main street and if anything different has opened.

All places are very much the same as the last time he was here.

Stopping in the centre of town Carr wanders the market. Finding a roasted lizard with a fresh bun to eat and to his delight a coconut, for a tasty drink.

Spotting a place in view of the tax building, he takes a seat on a large planter. Built in the middle of the road inset from the main corner.

Back against a tree he watches the many different people go about their business while enjoying his crispy lizard, and coconut milk.

One by one the market vendors cover their wares closing for the night.

From the north side of the targeted building, a dozen of King Darvel's horsemen escort a fancy carriage towards the north gate.

Carr begins to panic thinking the collection is headed for the castle.

Watching the carriage bounce along, between two long L-shaped barracks, Carr breathes a sigh of relief. Noticing the carriage is light and only being taken to the King's west-side stable, to be stowed.

Turning his attention back to the finely built, two-storey, stone bricked building. Its' tall thin windows, on both levels are too narrow for him to slide through, easily; only naked might he make it. Heavy well-crafted double wooden doors are set into the building's stonework atop of five grey marble slab steps. The lock of the door isn't a problem, not knowing how many guards wait on the other side is.

Three preteen boys run past Carr, yelling insults to each other in an apparent foot race, drawing lots of attention. Including a lone sentry, stationed on the roof of the building.

"Hmm…" Carr thinks watching the guard. "What goes up has to come down. Somehow?" Assuming there must be some kind of door up there Carr thinks about the best way to get to the roof. Seeing a street to investigate, behind the shops lining the west side, he takes his time eating allowing the sunset.

Casing the surrounding buildings Carr sees one that intrigues him; One that provides a place to sleep with a view of the tax buildings. A two storey wood and plaster Inn right across the street. Though both buildings are across from the barracks Carr doesn't worry, as the barracks have no windows, and the night's shadows will help conceal him.

A group of guards headed to the barracks take notice of Carr, nearing him one asks. "And what are you, up too?"

Turning sharply, Carr's a little surprised to see the group, identifying two of them as the men from the main gate. "I was wondering how much a room costs at this Inn." Pointing to the establishment.

One of the men coldly replies. "That place is too nice for the likes of you."

The old gate guard adds. "Ah. The Inn keeper will take one look at you and say the rooms are full."

"I see." Carr quietly replies.

The stable-boy informed the guards that Carr's headed for Qulun. So another of the men informs him. "There's a group of mercenaries staying at the Blarney Chicken tonight. They're headed for the Qulun Territory."

Almost forgetting, Carr answers. "Hmm, oh, yeah? Thanks, I still need a good drink."

The guards move on figuring the young man will be knocking at death's door before year's end.

As darkness falls a pair of men with long poles work the central part of the city. Hooking lanterns with their poles from tall wooden posts. Lowering them to fill with oil, light and return the lit lanterns to the post.

Before they light the area Carr's in, he slips between two of the western shops, to the rear street.

Casually walking past the rear of the target building Carr thinks. "Well the south alleyway looks like there's enough room to throw a grappling hook."

Double iron doors protect the ground level back entrance. An orange glow of torchlight outlines the doors. Carr can see that the doors are definitely barred from the inside.

He wants to peek through the door cracks but the rooftop sentry is observing his actions.

Rounding the corner and headed towards the main street Carr sees the windows to the upper floor of the Inn are dark, and hopes they are empty.

Crossing the main street Carr glances south seeing the two men are now starting to illuminate the area he was sitting in. Taking a second look he spots a pair of guards patrolling the main street.

Entering the dimly lit Inn Carr doesn't see anything too special about the establishment, nicely decorated with simple things.

Standing behind a small counter right of the entrance, an observant older woman softly greets him "Good Evening young man. Will you be requiring a room for the night?"

"Good Evening." Replies Carr glancing over the still pretty, fifty plus woman. "Yes I do." Smiling friendly he walks over to her. "I see you have rooms up front. Are they available for the night?" Feeling examined, he adds. "I'd hate to miss anything exciting, or at least amusing."

The woman knows he's up to something. "Oh, I'm sorry those rooms are rented to a family."

"Oh, that's too bad." Carr noticeable hesitates while rethinking his plan.

She leans forward suggesting in a subtle knowing tone. "There is a side room with a view of the street. Including..." Saying no more just motioning with her eyes to the tax building.

Nervous of what the woman suspects and wants Carr attempts to deceive her. "Kind woman I'm just looking for a comfortable bed before heading off to battle in the Qulon Territories."

Knowing he's lying she corrects him before asking. "You meant Qulun, but very brave of you. So, who are you siding with?" Winking once at him, for catching him in a tale.

Not even sure where the territory lies, he's got no clue what the fight is over or between who. Managing to blurt out. "Well I'm sure, you don't agree with what happened either. So I'm gonna side with them."

Holding back a laugh at his attempt to keep his cover, she tells him how it is. "If I was a child or drunk that might have worked on me." She sees worry in the young rogue's eyes. "Now and again someone will come in requesting the front rooms just for a short stay. They show up at odd hours keeping to themselves speaking with a silk tongue."

Carr notes. "Well this is an Inn."

She grins slyly motioning with her eyes again. "That is just a building with a lot of valuables in it."

Busted Carr asks. "Are you willing to accept gold for a still tongue?"

Happy he's seen the light she answers. "You know in the thirty years that building has been there. Only one skilled thief has managed to get in and out unseen. The rest, if not giving up the idea, just from the number of men housed in the two barracks. Have died entering or been stuck in the dungeon."

Thinking she's been here a long time Carr digs into his coin pouch. "So I take it you don't have any faith I'll succeed? But are willing to watch me try."

Finding three gold, are the only coins of value he puts them on the counter. "What will this buy me?"

"Oh, I'll certainly watch." She says smiling. "This one will pay for the room." Placing one of the gold in a lockable ornately inlayed box. Sliding the other two into a pocket." These, a very generous tip. My silence if you make it out, alive will cost more."

Not thinking clearly. "I've only six silver and a couple dozen copper left." He sees she's got something else in mind. "Or a piece of the take."

"Ah, what a smart young man." She winks at him. "If you were a little older I'd have a perfect task for you, but if you make it out. I'm sure the sparkle of a few good gems would make me forget all about you."

Thinking he's old enough, but doesn't know what she really wants Carr says. "I would be glad to deliver either and I'm sure I'm skilled enough to."

Finding the young man amusing she says. "The gems will do." Retrieving a skeleton key she steps from behind the counter. "Allow me to show you to your room."

"Sure." Carr simply replies, following her up a wide sturdy wooden staircase. Wondering if the woman is more devious the she appears.

Turning right at the top they pass the two doors to the front rooms and two rooms facing the back. Except for the squeaky floorboards the upper level is very quiet.

Stopping at the end of the short hall she unlocks a door, pointing out. "If you're a nervous sleeper the door can be locked from the inside." Stepping aside to let Carr in.

Carr enters the tiny room barely illuminated by a small window. The only furniture is an old heavy bed with straw mattress, no bedding.

He comments turning to her, "Hey, there's not even a pot to p..." but she's not there. "Oo, kay." Figuring this is her plan to rent out the worst room, Carr shrugs. "Well it's a good thing I didn't come here to actually sleep." Standing on the bed he pushes open the small door covering the window then sticks his head outside checking the view.

The window looks into the space between the neighboring shop. The back of the Inn is fenced in and from it the sounds of chickens. Telling Carr that there's probably a rooster, to wake him with the town guards, in case he actually falls asleep here.

There is a partial view of the stone building, including two windows and if he stretches out far enough, the edge of the main doors.

Glimpsing the lone sentry patrolling the rooftop Carr ducks back. Having seen the upper window lit he waits patiently for the man to pass.

Easing his face back out he sees the guard is sitting on the corner, facing the northwest skies.

Looking to the upper floor window, there's a definite silhouette of a round man sitting.

Concluding in his head "Ah, that must be the Lord, probably writing out all that was collected."

The sound of hollow metal scrapping on stone causes Carr to look up. The guard has taken his helmet off and appears to be searching his tunic.

Carr watches thinking what a perfect shot he could have on this guy. The man pulls out something small with a tiny pouch. Carr recognizes the object as a pipe.

"Alright." Carr ducks in the room dropping his backpack and sword on the bed, while sizing up the window opening.

Deciding it's big enough to sit in, he grabs up his bow and a single arrow; leaving the rest leaning close to the window.

Maneuvering his armored body out he's able to rest a foot on the rounded wood framework of the Inn's exterior. Catching his right foot under a thick rail making up the bed's headboard. He gets both arms out, putting the small of his back firmly against the window frame. Cautiously placing the arrow in the bow. He struggles drawing the string while trying to keep himself from falling out.

Igniting a splinter of wood with a lantern the guard uses it to light tobacco, in the pipe.

With legs jerking and twitching maintaining his stance, Carr manages to draw the bow as far as possible, shakily sighting up the guards back. Focusing on plunging the arrow through the back into the heart.

Sitting back puffing on the pipe the roof top guard watches the heavens. The light in the second floor window goes out.

Staying as steady as possible Carr takes a deep breath. Exhaling he releases the arrow.

The agile seasoned guard hears the snap of the bowstring hopping up and turning; the arrow pierces the man's throat straight through.

Carr's eyes widen amazed by the spectacular hit. The guard gargles trying to call out. Grabbing at the arrow as his body collapses onto the rooftop quickly draining out his lifeforce.

Excited Carr pumps the bow in his fist uttering a soft. "Yah." Not concentrating he looses the foothold on the bed.

Falling out the window Carr hits the ground hard, on his left side. Sore but still thrilled about the shot he picks himself up.

Taking a second to examine his bow, seeming okay he creeps to the street to see if anyone had noticed. A group of men standing around the north gate are too far away to have heard anything. As far to the south that he can see is void of any movement.

Feeling confident he calmly walks back into the Inn waving to the woman as he heads up the stairs.

She watches him curiously not too surprised to see him walking through the front door, having just heard a thump on the ground.

In the room Carr sets the bow aside, removing his cloak and rations from the pack.

Tying the hemp rope tightly to the grappling hook he returns it to the pack.

Slinging the long-sword across his back, he grabs the pack and heads downstairs.

Hearing him descending the woman jests. "Decided to take the stairs?"

Carr's cheeks turn a light shade of pink, too embarrassed to speak he just grins at her.

Stumbling missing the last step, turns his face bright red.

"Good Luck." She utters laughing under her breath, as Carr pushes instead of pulling on the door trying to leave.

Carr hesitates to calm, responding to her. "Thanks, I'll be alright I'm just eager to get started." Pulling open the door he exits.

Shaking her head at the foolish young thief she watches him cross the street and slip into the shadows of tax buildings' alleyway.

Immediately Carr takes the rope and hook out, checking the rear of the building, nobody in sight.

Creeping up to the front for one last check of the main street.

"Bang. Bang. Bang." Pounds a street patrolling guard on the front door of the building.

Carr drops to the ground skinnying up to the building's edge focused on the main street.

"It's Harland." Calls out the guard to the men on the inside of the building. "Alright."

The guard returns to his rounds joined by another sentry, both men casually walk by the alleyway, talking about favorite ales.

One man looks right down the alley. Carr's sure he was seen but stays still closing an eye. The woman watching from the Inn thinks he's been spotted too.

Not seeing him at all the guard continues to chat as they walk on.

Carr crawls to the street to see where the guards go.

Seeing Carr's hairy head pop out ground level from the shadows causes the woman to snicker.

They continue south towards the main gates. Carr feels safe that the guards won't be back for a while. Getting up he readies himself to toss the grappling hook onto the roof.

Holding the coil of rope loosely in his left hand he starts twirling the hook in the right. Letting go, the hook sails up, just not high enough. Not wanting the hook to make too much noise coming down Carr gets under it thinking he can catch it.

Connecting with the stonewall, the hook alters course one of its dull metal prongs clips Carr's forehead and skids off his chest-plate lightly thudding on the ground.

Touching the point of impact he checks if it's bleeding. Just another bruise, so he grabs the rope and hook for a second attempt.

This time the hook rather quietly lands on the roof.

Landing on the dead guard the hook rolls off, onto the roof.

Pulling the rope back the hook grapples the dead man's thigh.

The rope feels snug so Carr plants his feet against the buildings' stonewall. Pulling himself up; a very short distance as the body slides. Putting Carr's back onto the ground and the man's body against the roof's raised edge.

Standing Carr pulls hard on the rope it doesn't move. To make certain Carr jerks really hard, the hook tears into the dead man's pant leg.

Hoping that he doesn't slide down again Carr starts scaling the wall.

The mason's work is excellent leaving very little edge for Carr to catch his feet on.

Catching on quickly Carr uses mostly his arms to swiftly reach the top before strength gives out.

Tossing his leg over the top edge he rolls onto the roof. Seeing the body that helped him he grins slyly.

Carr quickly pulls up and coils the rope. Tucking the rope and hook back into his pack.

Taking the helmet off the wall Carr sits the man back up putting his helmet on. Leaving the body to look as though merely sleeping.

Investigating the area Carr sees a flat hatch at the back of the roof.

Bending down he places an ear to the hatch.

Sounding quiet he opens it slightly, seeing a tight room with a ladder going down; descending between two rows of shelving; one side is loaded with soaps and cleaning supplies. Bedding on the other side, mainly thick blankets.

Across from the ladder a narrow doorway highlighted by lantern light.

At the bottom he peeks through the cracks: just a stride or two away a grand marble staircase.

Following the matching rails right along an open landing there can be seen two carved wooden doors along the west wall. The end door leading to the room he saw the silhouette in.

The left side mirrors the right except for a guard leaning on the railing looking tired.

Planning his next move, room searches, starting to the far right. Coldly thinking he may have to take another man's life.

Climbing the ladder he takes the daggers out stabbing a bar of soap onto each blade. Clutching a downward facing dagger in each hand he carefully stretches his arms out, placing his fists on the opposite wall, bracing himself.

Stepping up one ladder rung at a time Carr makes his way high enough to hide his feet in the shadows.

Vibrating his fists he loosens the bars of soap dropping them. Making just enough noise to attract the nearby guard. Not enough to wake anyone sleeping or listening elsewhere in the building.

The noise catches the ear of the guard, who stares right at the tiny room. Standing tall he steps towards the door asking in a rough voice "That you, Sandy?" hearing no reply or further sound he mutters. "Rats." Thinking a rodent is in there.

Carr's body trembles at the sound of rats. Wondering if he's been found out and not sure how much longer he can keep still, maintaining his awkward position.

Taking up an iron mace the guard readies for something furry to scurry, gripping the door handle.

Jerking the door open the guard scans the floor seeing the bars of soap.

Nerves holding up well, Carr worries of slipping as his knuckles grind into the stonework.

The guard glances at the shelf the bars came from while bending down to pick them up.

Carr's chance to take him out, letting himself fall.

The guard sees him but doesn't even have a second to get out of the way.

Hitting the guard hard, slamming the man's head onto the stone floor. Carr lands on top piercing the man's back with one of his the daggers. The other scrapes across the guard's heavy leather tunic. The iron mace makes only a minor clang as it hits stone, still gripped tightly in the wielders hand.

Carr quickly raises his free dagger to separate the guard's spine when he realizes the man's out cold.

Laying still he surveys the second floor landing, waiting to see if any have been alerted by the sounds.

The sounds stirred some from their slumber but with no further noise they drift back to sleep.

Quietly Carr pulls the man's legs inside. Using washrags Carr binds and gags the guard. Noticing the growing welt on the man's forehead he's sure to be out for sometime.

Closing the door to the tiny room he heads straight for the second door on the right.

Following the landing, as it over looks the stairwell and the bottom landing. Only a few steps away from it a set of shut and latched, engraved wooden doors.

At the end of the upper landings there's arrow slits in the east wall.

Cautiously peering through the arrow slits into the main entrance hall. A single sentry stands; in the middle of the room humming a tune keeping watch on the main doors.

Two other doors are set into the wall opposite of each other. Not seen but sure the doors to the staircase are directly behind the humming male.

The masonry work is exceptional but the hall is void of furnishings accept for expensive oil lanterns. Hung on the walls between each doorway.

Beginning with the first room of interest he listens to the door turning the doorknob, the room is quiet and locked.

Removing his family lock picks, Carr examines the lock's keyhole and smiles. As his special master key, will certainly work on this lock. As they were both made by the same person.

Easily unlocking the door he slips into a dark office. The only light is from windows on the east and south walls.

A slate fireplace takes up most of the west wall, with a curtain, draped ceiling to floor, covering the remaining section.

Tapestries of four unknown family crests hang on the sidewalls.

Center of the room close to the east wall a large desk covered in ledgers scrolls and parchments.

In the corners of the east wall stand tall, detailed corner cabinets. Both filled with books papers and assorted bric a brac.

Seeing a couple animal figures Carr reminds himself to take only things small and valuable.

Nothing fitting that description the desk is searched, drawer by drawer checking for secret compartments as he goes.

Finding nothing useful Carr sits back in a desk chair surveying the room.

Thinking. "There's got to be something of value in here perhaps a hidden door." His eyes focus on the curtain beside the fireplace.

Over to the curtain, he pulls it aside to see a door.

Placing his ear up to it, to hear snoring coming from the other side.

Trying the door, it opens, peeking in to see a dark but noticeably lavish, bedchamber.

Directly in front of a fancy mirrored washstand and by the smell, somebody has a recently used pee pot.

Entering he squeezes past the washstand closing the door behind.

The room is expensively furnished Carr can smell actual wood-stain.

Partially illuminated by a shaded window a grand canopy bed, located centrally against the west wall, with a round snoring man in it. On both sides of the bed are nightstands.

To Carr's right a fireplace mirrors the first room and is joined by a common flue. Just past that the door back to the landing; he can see that the door key is in the lock. Next to the window an armoire and on the opposite wall an actual closet.

Starting with the armoire he opens the top cabinet doors, inside hangs a large suit of finely tailored leather armor and a matching soft boots. Needing a new pair Carr briefly compares them with his feet, being too small he puts them back.

Nothing else worthwhile he closes the doors and rummages the drawers, mainly bed linens, two pillows and a few horrid dressing gowns.

Braving an inspection of the adjacent nightstand, on it's top a drying pastry with a big bite out of it.

Inside a small drawer he finds a sheathed dagger, feeling jewels set into the handle he immediately adds it to his pack.

Creeping to the other nightstand the man stirs in his sleep Carr drops below the mattress.

The tax collector grunts and grumbles rolling over, Carr stays still. Within minutes the snoring starts again.

A lantern sitting behind a pitcher of water and a single goblet cover the nightstand. Feeling safe to proceed, Carr opens the stand's small drawer, only to find some parchments.

Turning to something he seldom gets to explore he enters the closet. A small space filled with fine clothes. Dozens of pants, shirts and coats hang on either side.

Catching his eye a short-sword with jewels set into its handle, in an elaborately engraved sheath. It hangs on an iron spike in the doorframe. Leaving little doubt that this is the short-sword Effim requested.

More on a whim Carr shoves it into the pack. The tip of the handle pokes out of the backpack.

Shelves below the hanging clothes are lined with socks and undergarments. Not owning any socks he helps himself to a few of the softest pairs.

Perking his interest even more than the fancy short sword. A leather covered wood chest sits concealed in the shadows under the sock shelf.

Kneeling, he feels the lid's lock. Pulling on the chest he smiles at how heavy it is.

Waiting to drag it forward as the fat man snores, to mask the trunk's sound as it scrapes on the floor.

Carr checks the dangling lock, not a problem for him having picked many, of this maker's locks.

Fiddling in the dark he picks the lock within a minute. Putting his picks away he's ready to open the chest wildly fascinated by what could be inside.

Easing the lock off and setting it aside, he pushes up the lid up. The box is nearing full of jewels, gems and jewelry.

"Well. Well. Well." Whispers Carr, looking over to the sleeping man. "Looks like somebody's starting a collection of their own. I wonder if the King is aware? I don't think so."

Grabbing a couple more pairs of socks he fills three with stones and gems. The last one slowly filled with nice jewelry filtered from the precious stones, noting. "No rings." Taking an extra moment to feel the contents. "No rings at all."

Tying knots on the ends of the socks he places them in the backpack, content if he finds nothing else the trip is well paid for.

Closing the chest he relocks it timing the click with a snore, and pushing the chest back.

Confident there's nothing more here to find he goes back out through the office relocking the door.

"Bang. Bang. Bang." Carr's heart almost stops, as the street guard pounds on the main doors.

"Who's there?" Dully asks the main hall guard. Having asked that question thousands of times.

Barely heard the reply. "Just Harland."

The hall guard finishes with. "All's quiet. Until you come banging. Not so damn loud." Grumbling to himself. "I don't care if he hates Lord Piate. That fat bastard sleeps through earthquakes. The rest of us have to sleep. Geez, How many times?..."

Raising a brow Carr smirks thinking. "Well if I don't find the rings soon. I'll just come back and help lighten Lord Pieate's ill gotten booty."

Crossing over to the north side, Carr stops making sure his captive is still unconscious.

Satisfied Carr takes a listen to the next door.

Sounding quiet, the door isn't locked or barred. He opens it enough to see it's the servants' quarters. Three women rest comfortably, nothing but foolish curiosity in there.

Checking the last door Carr realizes right away not to enter, sounds of different snoring mark the room as guards quarters. Backing away he widens the search, by heading downstairs.

Tip toeing to the bottom he sees there are narrow hallways on either side of the stairs. Not wanting to go into the main hall, Carr investigates the north hallway.

Ending at a door Carr checks before opening it.

On the other side the back entrance to the building, a single door on the north and south walls and in between the two narrow halls, another set of stairs descending to a cellar.

Looking down the stairs he sees a flickering light, off to the right.

Hesitating at the top he wonders. "Could be a trap. It's been almost easy. I can't believe, I'll be the second one to get out of here." Glancing at the rear doors. "It does make sense to locate heavy goods near an entrance." Taking a cautious minute he checks the other two unknown doors.

The south door leads to a well-stocked kitchen. The north door leads to a large room running from west to east the complete span of the first floor. Containing a few desks with a matching chair for each. A couple cabinets contain various books.

The only thing catching Carr's eye are the tapestries hanging on the walls. They seem to be all painted landscapes. Figuring it must be place for carrying out business or decisions, he decides to go down-stairs.

With extreme care on the stairs Carr stops before the bottom to check what's in the cellar. Not as big as building's main floor, the cellar is still fair in size. The unlit north part is being used for storage. Barrels, crates and sacks are piled in the center of the area, also lining sections of the walls in between a few cabinets.

Peeking around the stairwell wall into the illuminated southern portion. Iron bars imbedded into the floor and secured to an upper floor joist. Forming a caged off area, lit inside by a burning torch, and illuminating a guard sitting behind a desk.

Alarmed Carr pulls his face back, wondering. "Was that guy sleeping?"

Cautiously taking a second look, the man's head is resting atop folded arms. "Oh perfect." Sure that the guard is sleeping Carr looks over the area.

The guard's helmet sits beside him on the desk. He slumbers peacefully in the rounded southeast corner. Behind him a mace and loaded crossbow lean against the wall.

Ending at the stairwell wall is another row of iron bars making up a second caged room inside the first.

Carr's eyes widen and a sly grin stretches across his face, seeing inside the second area. Lined against the west wall five chests each one different from the other. One is wooden the other four are mainly made of steel, wonderfully detailed and all have built in locks.

"I should go find a horse and wagon." Carr dreams knowing he'd struggle just to get the chests up the stairs. Let alone into a wagon for a trip across the mountains. "I sure could use one of those girdles of giant strength."

Studying his first problem the sleeping guard, too far in to be stabbed by his long-sword or a pole arm, if he had one.

Thinking he should've brought the bow he stares into the dark storage area.

Carr slips into the shadows to search for something useful to help take the guard out.

Immediately, piled high behind the stair wall furniture, benches, tables, and cabinets. Most of it, in better condition then what's in the farmhouse.

"No, not a girdle, I have to get me a scroll of teleportation. Oh, but, the wizards say, its too dangerous for a young thief. Don't wanna end up in a rock wall or a plane in hell." Quietly mumbling Carr searches dusty rows of shelves that line the remainder of the west wall. Filled with all kinds of things that he can't properly see or has time for, and nothing helpful.

A few barrels and crates are stacked in the corner. Smelling fruits and vegetables inside the containers he steps in front of a long tall cabinet.

Carr glances at the guard hoping the shadows are concealing enough. Quickly jerking open the door to avoid any squeaking, the smell of leather floats out. Feeling inside the dark cabinet, it seems to be filled with folded leather tunics.

No weapons seen walking between the stacks of supplies. Stopping at the last cabinet Carr's exposed to the stairwell and the guard if he wakes up.

Quickly opening the door he sighs to the sight of shelves full of ceramic, wood and glass containers, storing herbs and preserves.

Stepping back into the shadows Carr kneels behind a barrel easing his pack gently on the ground, thinking about the next move. "I think I can pick the lock without waking him. Can I take him out before he calls for help?"

Convinced the sound of the iron bar door opening will surely wake the guard. Carr readies as best as possible, quietly unsheathing the long-sword and taking only his favorite three lock tools.

Close to the stairs he sets down the pack and sheath incase of a hasty retreat.

Kneeling in front of the door lock, he rests the sword on the ground for quick retrieval. Adjusting position slightly, to keep an eye on the guard, while examining the inside of the keyhole.

From the parts inside he recognizes the maker but not the lock; Softly poking and pushing on the inner components, with tools in hand.

Quickly figuring out how it works, he glances at the man, obviously out Carr works the lock. The lock is stiff making it difficult to move and there's a tiny piece of metal acting as a stop. After a minute the lock's bolt starts to slide.

"Clack!" Echoes the lock as an inner spring retracts the bolt, seeming loud in the quiet cellar.

The guard stirs, with no time to waste Carr let's go of the picks.

Grabbing the sword and jumping to his feet he pushes open the iron-gate rushing in.

Blurry eyed the guard sees somebody's coming at him and franticly reaches for either of his weapons.

With blade cocked back Carr lines up the man as he grabs the mace while scrambling to stand and defend himself.

Carr swings out his blade hard and fast severing the guard's head from neck.

Stopping himself on the back wall Carr watches the man's head, bounce off the desk and roll across the caged area to the open gate. Blood sprays over the joists and walls, as the body collapses twitching on the floor. Knocking over a chair and crossbow, lunching its projectile; the bolt pierces a sack of grain, the mace tings hitting the ground.

Not hearing the ting Carr stands against the wall amazed at his own strike. Realizing the racket that was made he creeps over to the stairs gathering his picks from the floor.

Watching up the stairs for a couple minutes, not even a creak is heard. Taking his gear back into the first cage he sets it down beside the next doorway.

Checking the desk Carr finds a single key, trying it on the main gate lock. It works and the second looks the same as the first lock.

Unlocking the second gate, he pulls the door open.

Excited to be nearing his prize Carr dances over to gather the backpack and sword sheath, rubbing his dirty hands together. "Alright. Easy as one two, three, this booties for me."

With picks at the ready Carr sits in front of the wooden chest, the curious excitement causes him to fumble with the lock. After several frustrating attempts the lock opens. Carr pops the lid up and sighs, as the chest is full of copper coins. Shrugging he moves over to the next chest, cracking his knuckles before attempting the lock.

In a calmer state Carr pops the lock within a minute, inside are two heavy canvas bags.

Opening them, they're full of silver coins. Better, but not worth carrying for three days. Closing the lid he looks at the third.

Joking around he sniffs the middle chest's rounded lid. "It's gold I smell in there."

Quickly picking the lock, he sets the tools down. Pausing for effect to open the lid.

Inside two leather satchels with buckled ties. Like a kid on his birthday he fumbles with the ties, hoping for a wish to be filled.

Unbuckling them both, he grabs the buckles and pulls back both covers revealing something better.

One satchel almost overflows of gold coins, the other is over half full of platinum coins.

Trying to pick up the platinum satchel he knows he could carry it but only that.

Not sure what do take, he glances at the two other chests. Remembering he's supposed to be after a set of rings. Leaving the lid open he crawls over to the fourth, looking back at the platinum.

Thinking too much he wastes a few minutes opening the lock.

Inside lay many small leather pouches and canvas sacks. Wasting more time he opens each one, beginning with the pouches.

The first contains a strange sparkling powder it doesn't smell nice or familiar. Setting it aside he picks out another, filled with assorted sized pearls. Dragging the backpack over he reties the pouch and inside the pack it goes.

Delighted to see what else is in the last three. Each one contains assorted cut gems. Pleasing Carr further they're separated by size.

Hastily knotting the drawstrings he adds them to the pack. "The five to twenty gold bag. A twenty to fifty bag." Carr kisses the last one. "And a fifty to hundreds bag. I can retire this old armor for sure."

Checking out the canvas sacks, raw ore has been collected, silver, gold, and platinum. Nice but heavy and not needed.

Closing the lid he sees the powder still sitting there. Unsure if it has any value, he picks it up, being light in weight it gets added to the pack.

Turning to the last chest Carr sniffs it. Getting in front of the lock he puts an ear to the lid. "I could smell gold but I'm sure I can hear the sparkle of gems. This must be the royal jewelry box."

Cracking the lock Carr stretches out his arm to pat himself on the back.

Slowly opening the engraved lid the contents sparkle in the torchlight. A smile, like one seeing kittens play, crosses Carr's face. Viewing the heaping box of jewelry. He wants to examine every piece but doesn't have the time.

Taking the leather sack from his backpack. Carr tosses handfuls of jewelry into the sack while searching for the quested rings.

Concerned for time he barely sees what he's doing. The sack now round he has to stop in order to tie the bag, still no rings.

Adding the heavy bag to the pack Carr sifts through the still full chest. Thinking he may have to dump it out. Scraping up a monster, over extravagantly jeweled necklace; a small child could wear it as a dress. Amazed by the time and work that went into it he holds it up to his chest.

Snickering at himself he spots the rings, resting as they should, side by side.

Carr drops the weighted garment and grabs up the rings clutching them tight.

Reaching down his chest he pulls out a tiny pouch that hangs from his neck. It usually contains just his emergency platinum coin.

Barely seeing torchlight they're inserted and tucked back under the scale armor.

Patting his chest, he picks up his pack checking on its weight. Thinking he can handle another stone in weight he looks over the chests.

Having plenty of precious stones, he eyes up the gold. Returning the monster necklace and rapidly tossing the rest of the spilt jewelry back into its container, he closes it up.

Making some room in the pack he attaches the short sword and his own around the waist.

Taking a pair of socks he fills one with gold and the other with platinum, wedging them and the picks into the backpack.

Hoisting the heavy pack onto his back he closes the last chest.

Closing and locking the iron-gate while exiting he looks over the decapitated man.

Struggling with the backpack Carr takes the man's head and places it back onto its' shoulders.

Locking the first gate, he purposely snaps the key off in the lock.

Tackling the stairs with loaded back Carr breaks into a sweat, reaching the top.

"Bang! Bang! Bang!" pounds the patrolling guard at the main door.

"Pound, pound, pound." Goes Carr heart, grabbing wall to keep from falling back down the stairs.

Unbarring the rear doors Carr softly rests the two heavy wood beams on the floor.

Surveying the area behind the building, nothing is moving within his view.

Closing the doors behind, he heads for the alley.

Stopping to check the street he sees Harland, the loud banger, walking south with his guard buddy.

Carr waits until they cross the market. Glancing over at the Inn he notices the older woman seems to be watching for him.

Waiting motionless Carr contemplates. "I can't believe I got away with it. I'm getting good. Soon I'll be able to afford to build a keep, maybe on a cliff edge or opposite King Halford's Castle. I've definitely got to make a trip there after I get back. Maybe I can trick Ma into coming along… If she's not too mad."

Observing the Innkeeper. "Why is it women don't think I can do it. Well I can now certainly show them."

Checking on the street patrol, they're nowhere to be found. Feeling confidently cocky, Carr struts across the street. Straight into the Inn, quietly closing the door he approaches the woman.

Genuinely surprised she comments. "Did you get what you wanted? Or did you even get in?"

Carr turns resting the weighted pack on the counter, sliding his arms out he faces her.

As she curiously leans over to look at the backpack, Carr amazes even himself boldly planting a quick kiss on the woman's cheek.

Winking once he says. "I got exactly what I came for, and a wee bit more." Opening the pack

In no way offended by the young male, she states. "I never thought I'd be here to see the building burgled twice. The thief's guild even leaves that place alone. There hasn't been an attempt in over two years. Who are you?"

Opening the pouch of large gems he gladly replies. "Carr, Carr the Daring." Reaching in he grabs up several gems.

Studying Carr, she smiles. "Well Carr, you certainly are daring, or foolish. Either way I must congratulate you. My name is Makah, and something tells me our paths will cross in the future."

Placing the stones on the counter. "Oh yah. Well Makah will these buy silence."

Her eyes sparkle with the gems. "Oh yes, and far too generous." She says but still slips all the precious stones into her pocket.

Closing the pack. "Not to worry." Heaving the pack onto his back. "Now I must get a little sleep, but I was hoping you could wake me before the city gates are opened?"

"Not to worry." She points out. "The rooster in the pen out back will surely get you up."

Heading for the stairs. "Thank-you Makah, you're a wonderful being."

She slyly responds. "I certainly am. You get some sleep. You'll need to stay alert later today. Good luck Carr." Watching him pull his way up the stairs.

In the room he closes and latches the door.

Dropping the pack on the bed for a lumpy pillow.

Closing the window he removes the swords and hangs them from the bedpost.

Lying on the straw he fantasizes of how to spend his growing fortune.

"Er, Eee, Er, E, Err." The Inn rooster crows out inspiring other roosters into waking the city.

Sitting up too fast Carr's head spins, having only slept a few hours, attempting to get moving.

With no room left in the pack he straps the short-sword around the waist concealing it under the old tattered cloak.

Already getting warm with all that's worn Carr slings the bow and long-sword across his back. Then struggles to get the bulky pack in place.

Staggering down the hall with quiver in hand and tempting fate down the stairs Carr noisily leaves.

A lean, well, groomed man, of forty years comes out from behind the desk curious to whom is making the noise.

Sighting Carr he firmly points out. “Hey others are trying to sleep.”

Slowing up Carr apologizes. “I'm sorry good sir.” Stopping briefly at the bottom. “Sorry just in a hurry. Tell Makah I said thanks again.”

“Makah?” Confused the man looks over Carr trying to remember his face. “Who are you?”

Unsure if he pronounced her name correctly. “The pretty older women, she checked me in last night.” Carr backs towards the door.

The man knows not, pointing out. “I only check people in and I lock the front doors after seven.”

Responding with his hand on the door. “Well, I paid her a gold.” Opening the door slightly he hesitates raising a complaint. “And I got a bed with no linens or a pot to piss in.”

The man glances up to where that room is located. “I don't rent out that room.” Stepping back to check his coin box. “Who'd you say you were?”

Unsure of what's going on and just wanting to get out of Monsteil Carr blurts out. “It's, ah, James Cabe.” Ducking out the door he heads for the public stables.

The true Innkeeper finding an extra gold in his box doesn't pursue the matter, right away.

Briskly making his way across the city, its' guards are readying to change shifts.

Waking guards in the tax building have found the man left tied up.

Approaching the barn he can see the stable-boy is bringing Bressi out. Beyond the stable, the main gates are opening.

The bodies of Carr's victims have been found and Lord Piate has been woken.

“Good morning.” Carr greets the male, digging out his coin pouch. “Thank-you so much for having her ready. Here,” handing the man the six silver coins. "Keep it, get yourself something." Patting Bressi he straps the quiver onto the saddle.

"O, thanks." He replies pocketing the coins, to help Carr up. "It's a pleasure to take care of such a beautiful horse, how long have you had her?"

"Thanks again." Carr appreciates the boost. "I've had her seven years."

Guards from the tax building are running out into the street deciding who should go where.

Still in a fog the Innkeeper enters the street asking the men. "What's going on?"

One of the guards asks him. "Did you see anyone strange around here last night?"

Automatically the Innkeeper thinks of Carr, keeping his reply simple he points to the south. "A scruffy young human male with a heavy backpack, headed that way a few minutes ago."

"Right." The guard utters, thanking the Innkeeper he sends a man running for the south gate to warn them to close it. Another is sent to the barracks to rally the men. Then tells a servant to inform the Lord of the events so far, before running for the gate.

The stable-boy kindly says. "Well I hope Bressi stays with you several more."

"Me too." Carr utters, directing Bressi towards the main gate. "I hope you have a pleasant day."

"Yah" the stable-boy waves to them. "Take care."

Spotting a rider leaving the stables the racing guard yells out repeatedly. "Stop! Him! Close! Gate!"

The guard following behind glimpses a distant rider, turning around he runs back yelling. "Horse! Men! Now!"

Carr hears the first man and gets Bressi to run. Seeing this causes the guards to scramble closing the heavy hinged steel doors of the city walls.

Archers hastily grab and fire arrows not taking the time to aim properly.

Bressi clears the doors with ease.

Launching their second round of arrows at the fleeing pair, one scrapes across Bressi's rump leaving but a scratch. Two pierce the backpack but are stopped by the contents.

The last arrows are fired a second too late as Bressi gallops out of range.

Passing the last of the fields Carr glances back seeing no followers yet, he smiles confident he's gotten away with his caper.

Back in the city four horsemen begin a pursuit while six more are but a few minutes from being ready and another dozen horses are being saddled.

At the mountain pass Carr and Bressi slow to navigate the rough terrain, beginning the long twisting ascent out of Darvel's territory.

Reaching a section Carr has to lead Bressi he looks out to see the four horsemen are quickly reaching the base of the pass. Along the road he sees six are behind them and a dozen riders are clearing the gates.

Mildly concerned about the future Carr thinks of how to elude the pursuing riders.

Thinking about the path happened upon days past, he wonders if he can find an alternate path to it from this side. Getting a view of the landscape he notices a ridge leading east around the nearest peak.

Higher up the pass a small animal trail becomes visible, running towards the ridgeline.

Taking the almost empty flask of water from the saddlebag, and the quiver of arrows. "Bressi girl you go home." He talks calmly to the horse directing the way. "Go home to Ma. Get the honey oats. Go on then." They have none but the horse responds continuing onward.

Carr gently makes his way through the first section of the barely recognizable trail.

Looking back occasionally to make sure he's not leaving any obvious signs of a side trip; Hoping that no matter what Bressi, doesn't stop, alerting the men that he's taken the alternate route.

As the path opens up into light brush, Carr runs where possible and darts across open sections.

Traversing the mountainside isn't difficult, just tiring being weighted down.

Late afternoon; despite the cool breezes Carr begins to overheat; his muscles vibrate and burn.

Holding up in a small group of trees and brush he quickly drops the backpack. Leaning the bow, quiver and long-sword against a fallen tree, to peels off the cloak and toss it aside.

Noticing the arrows stuck in the pack he plucks them out. Satisfied the contents are not going to spill out he rests his butt on the fallen tree causing it to bend. Exhausted he doesn't care if it hit ground, he'd happily go with it.

Drinking the last of the water Carr remembers his rations aren't with him. Sighing he folds over resting his chest on his lap; Allowing his arms and head to relax closing his eyes listening to the wind carry through the foliage.

Chapter Three
Getting Home

"Hey thief!" barks someone.

Feeling poked in the throat Carr opens his eyes seeing his own cold, steel blade under the chin. The hilt firmly grasped in the gauntlet of a tall, sturdy guard, that's studying him.

A younger bearded male stands off to the side; Astonished that some young punk dared and almost succeeded in stealing from their King Darvel.

The guard with the sword applies pressure to the blade asking. "Is that all you took?" pointing to the backpack.

The second man kneels to examine its contents.

Looking the man in the eye, Carr replies. "Yeah."

The tall guard sternly asks. "Did you kill the men?"

The second man looks over waiting for a response, to see Carr just nods yes, getting agitated he asks. "We gonna kill him?"

Poking Carr's throat the guard attempts to figure something out. "We were told a lone male broke into King Darvel's Affairs building, stealing the entire tax collection, and killed a few men in doing so."

Carr attempts to explain.

"Sshhh." The guard hushes him continuing his thought. "We were the first of the riders on your butt, and found your horse grazing along the trail. It's saddlebags empty, two shoes thrown and a bad split in one of the hooves. My question for you is, how many of you thieves were involved?"

Maintaining eye contact Carr answers in a raspy voice. "Just me."

"He's liein." Utters the second man. "Sir, its' just a regular pack. And there's only a small part of what was told to be stolen."

"That's the problem Philip." The guard points out. "Only one horse left the city. There's no way that horse could carry the whole collection. I'd say from the split hoof, the horse was struggling to carry our thief and his stolen goods. Somebody's lying to us and I haven't seen signs of anyone else out here."

Philip stands, unsure of the problem he queries. "What are you saying?'

Carr utters. "Piate is the thief."

A grin forms on the guard's lips hearing that and says to Philip. "There it is. There's more to the story than we're aware." Easing pressure off the blade. "What have you to say? That will save your butt."

"I didn't come to steal the collection." Carr states the facts honestly. "I came for two rings, by myself. In the Lord's bedchambers, I found a chest. Over flowing with jewelry and precious stones."

Philip gruffly dismisses him remarking. "So…He gets paid well. What were you doing in his bed chambers, anyways?"

The tall guard rolls his eyes. " Go on. Tell me what you're getting at?"

Seeing that, Carr goes on. "It looks like the Lord has been stealing for a long time, to have what I saw. It sounds like, I'm being used as cover for the whole collection going missing."

"Ahh." Not believing him Philip suggests. "Truth or not lets kill him and take the stash for ourselves."

"If I wasn't a sworn officer, I'd be tempted." Tapping the bottom of Carr's jaw with the sword tip, the guard, points out. "What the both of you aren't aware of is… Lord Piate and a few of his men, are being watched. The King is always concerned about theft from his own people. For the last few months a couple of his selected men have been seen around the city spending more than they earn. So young thief you're life cold be spared if we take you back to the King to plead your case. Perhaps you'll only be put in prison or maybe one of the work gangs for his Majesty's mines."

Not what Carr considers as a way to live out his life, he sighs. "I guess I don't have any real choice, if I want to live."

"See that Philip, he can be reasonable." The guard grins seeing praise and reward in his future. Hoping if it's true that Lord Piate is stealing, there's a chance for advancement, if he can bring back the thief alive. "Bind his hand's and we'll take him back to King Darvel. He'll decide the thief's fate."

"Alright." Sighs Philip sliding his satchel forward. "I don't think he's worth the effort."

Becoming jittery Carr is thinking about bolting, risking a cut on the neck. Already becoming dark he'll be able to find cover.

"Philip, you're thinking to small." The man continues his thought. "If the Lord is crooked. Us using this thief, we'll be rewarded."

Digging for a leather strap Philip pleads. "My God man there's plenty reward just sittin' here."

Chuckling the man points out. "Perhaps us returning what was only taken with the live thief and his story. Darvel will see our honesty and loyalty to his Kingdom. If the Lord is guilty he'll surely be put to death and King Darvel will need to find a new man to collect taxes. Who better, then men he can trust."

Pulling out a strap Philip processes the thought, walking towards Carr it sinks in. "Oh, I see. Tibor I knew there was a reason I listen to you. You become the new tax collector, I your captain and we compensate ourselves."

Carr can't argue with that logic. "I'd do it."

"Bet you would." Tibor motions to Philip to bind Carr. "Play nice, thief and maybe I'll spring you from jail once and awhile. I'm sure someday I could make use of your skills."

Starting to stick his hands out Carr utters. "Maybe someday…" Seizing the last good opportunity he flips backwards off the trunk landing on his feet and tears off. The tip of the sword only scratches his chin.

Being younger Philip gives chase still clutching the leather strap.

Tibor not wanting anything to happen to the treasure picks up the backpack and uses Carr's long-sword as a walking stick briskly following. Not too worried knowing where Carr's running too.

So do two other beings, sitting higher on the mountain, a pair of giants. With nothing better to do, they have been watching all day.

Fearing capture over death Carr races through the mountainside brush, ducking and dodging leading the men further east. Philip stays close but just can't gain any distance.

Traveling more than a league over the rough terrain Carr can't hear his footfalls over his pounding heart and aching lungs.

Glancing back Philip is still in pursuit. Looking forward a knee high tree root ahead and no time to alter course.

Carr jumps, easily clearing it. There just isn't any ground on the other side, Carr's eyes widen as he sails over a deep fissure in the mountainside.

The level of ground is higher on the other side. Slamming hard into the rocky edge with the bottom of his upper leg coverings. A couple of scale tips crack and scrape off. His left arm partially protects his face as the body hits ground skidding head first across a small clearing into a shrub.

Only seeing Carr jump over the root Philip leaps it too, yelping a high pitch, noticing the fissure below.

Slamming chest height in to the rock surface. Clutching mitts full of grass, and weeds he holds on.

Sore and wheezing Carr rolls over to see Philip pulling himself up. Thumping pain in Carr's legs make it hard for him to stand.

Noticeable winded Philip struggles to upright himself. Panting Carr knows he can't run any farther and Philip's griping the hilt of his bastard-sword, this can only end with spilt blood. Missing the long-sword Carr draws his newly acquired short-sword.

High up and impressed the humans cleared the fissure the giants elbow one another, to pay attention. Both hoping an entertaining fight will take place.

Still half a league back Tibor tires from the heavy pack. Not wanting to leave it he slows up. Certain Philip has cornered or killed the thief at the fissure.

Sweaty, sore and short of breath the pair square off, sizing each other up. Carr recalls lessons taught in using a short blade, choosing to wait for his foe to make the first move.

Clearly agitated Philip feels he has a superior weapon and only needs a second.

Rushing in, Philip attempts to hack off Carr's arm. Leaning back Carr deflects the blade with his, avoiding the strike.

Philip pivots following through, for a second swing. Carr jumps to the side slashing low, narrowly missed by Philips blade.

Carr's blade cuts into Philip's pants leaving a very minor cut to the side of his knee.

Angered by the nick, Philip begins a flurry of wild swings. Carr does his best to block and dodge the hefty blade.

Escaping another swing Philip kicks Carr in the stomach. Pushed back a step but not hurt, Carr steps back further.

Needing a breather Philip steps back, frustrated with the young thief.

Having heard the distant sound of clashing metal Tibor picks up his pace again.

Focused on the fight the giants don't see Tibor approaching.

Out thinking Carr, Philip swiftly steps forward swinging up, Carr automatically attempts to block. The heavier sword knocks the short-sword free of Carr's hand landing behind.

Seeing his chance Philip aggressively attacks.

Carr tries to keep some distance eluding the dangerous advances.

Closing in, barely able to make out the dueling pair Tibor thinks his partner has it under control.

Drawing a dagger Carr comes close to losing a nose, jumping aside.

Philip turns striking down as Carr throws the dagger: missing Philip's head. The blade of the bastard-sword chops through the scale armor slicing into the left, fleshy shoulder stopping the blade with the collarbone.

In pain Carr cries out, blood splatters across their faces as Philip pulls his sword out grinning.

Philip attempts to thrust the sword through, Carr pivots out of the way digging for the second dagger.

Immediately Philip turns swinging for Carr's stomach. Hopping back Carr watches the bastard-sword tip skip across the scales. The force of the blade pulls its wielder. Philip's arms continue to move back twisting himself off balance.

Staggering away Philip loses control tossing his weapon before hitting the ground. The back of his shoulder connects with a rock as his body flops to the ground. The bastard-sword skips off the ground then down the fissure, tinging its way to the bottom.

Trying to get up Philip shakes his head; Carr hesitates noticing something's not right. A look of panic crosses the man's face, as all his muscles stiffen.

Excited by the spectacle and wondering why Carr doesn't finish the man, one of the giants almost yells it out, stopped by his buddy.

Reaching the fissure Tibor sees they're on the other-side. Quiet and curious he watches from the shadows removing his gauntlets.

Clenching his jaw tight enough to crack bad teeth, Philip's body totally stiffens, jerking about several times. The panicked look washes off his face, with all colour. Philip collapses exhausting out his last breath.

Wondering what happened all stare motionless at Philip. Carr looks curiously up to the heavens, inspiring the others.

Cautiously approaching Philip, Carr mumbles. "What the hell?" Bending in he pinches the man's ear, checking for a reaction. "What happened?"

Feeling the blood run from the pulsating wound down his body. "I've got the worst of it..?" Now feeling watched he thinks. "Maybe there's a magic-user out there. I wonder what they'd want with me?" Trying not to look obvious Carr scans the surroundings seeing a silhouette across the fissure.

Carr speaks hoping to figure out who is standing there. "Thanks, but it wasn't needed. I had him, right where I wanted him."

"It wasn't me." Tibor utters revealing himself, as he steps from the shadows.

Almost forgetting about him the giants nod, seeing more entertainment.

Figuring he's got a minute Carr looks for a weapon. "Hey. I didn't kill your friend."

"I saw." Tibor still wants to bring him in breathing. "But no one is going to believe it. Your charges will be the murder of three of the King's men and grandous theft. I'm sure you didn't kill Philip. I am, however gonna lay a beaten on you for it. Then your gonna help get his body back."

Spotting the short-sword Carr inches towards it. "You must really want to be the collector?"

"Aye." Tibor tries to make a deal. "Like I said before, plead your case. I'll see that you're only jailed, instead of being put to death."

Bending down to pick up the sword Carr replies. "I'd rather be put to death."

Realizing the thief is about to flee again, Tibor places a magical ring on his finger uttering. "Give it up thief. Hey, I'm not chasing you all over this mountainside."

Inserting the sword into its sheath Carr remarks. "Then don't." With a smile and a wave good-bye he takes off.

Backing up Tibor runs at the tree root, lifting off the ground by the aid of the magic ring.

Springing off the root he easily clears the fissure even with the heavy pack. Landing squarely he drops the old long-sword and races after Carr and quickly gains ground.

Glancing back Carr's amazed to see how fast Tibor is. Unable to out run him, Carr draws the sword while turning to face Tibor.

Noticing Carr turning to attack, Tibor leaps through the air.

Catching Carr off guard, Tibor lands a flying forearm to Carr's chest. As they go down the blade of the short-sword slices across Tibor's fingers.

With the added weight of the pack Tibor lands hard, almost cracking both their ribs. Hitting the ground the short-sword is tossed and Tibor's ring falls off unnoticed.

Crossing Carr's arms over his chest, Tibor pins them, then knells on top. "Had to run." He says angry, laying a flurry of punches to Carr's head. "Got Philip killed! Ran again! Stupid

Bastard! I hope you, like pain, cause that's, what you're gonna get, for the rest, of your life!"

Satisfied with the beating Tibor contends with his pinned satchel to retrieve a leather strap. Defeated Carr lays there wondering again, what's better.

Discouraged by no more swordplay, one of the giants wants to help. Holding a rock in one hand he points at Tibor. His buddy takes the rock and sets it down. Being curious to see if the small human can escape before getting to the city.

Finding a strap Tibor binds Carr's wrists. "Now we're going back for Philip's body. You're responsible for his death you can carry him."

Carr questions. "With my hands tied?"

Forcing Carr up by his wrists Tibor responds. "He can hang over your shoulder. Now let's go."

Returning Tibor notices he's lost his ring, if it wasn't dark he'd go looking for it. Annoyed he shoves Carr aside to pick up Philip's body. Folding him over Carr's right shoulder. He pushes Carr to continue east knowing a different way to get off the mountain.

Seeing the long-sword Tibor picks it up reusing it as a walking stick.

Slowly navigating the path, weighted down Carr struggles passing over a log he easily cleared twice.

Feeling dizzy Tibor wipes sweat from his brow.

Getting over the log Carr carries on. Tibor has to force his legs to move. Hoisting a leg over the log Tibor losses balance, crashing to the ground.

Carr turns to see what happened.

Tibor is convulsing like Philip did.

"Hey!" Carr calls to Tibor. "Hey, you alright?"

The only reply from Tibor is his dying breath.

Concerned for his own wellbeing Carr looks about approaching Tibor. Kicking Tibor's nose, seeing no movement he drops Philip's body.

Using his teeth he unties the leather strap.

Free and curious Carr searches their bodies for signs of death. Finding only the cuts on Tibor's fingers and barely a cut on Philip's leg.

Taking the backpack off Tibor, Carr gingerly seats the strap over the wounded left shoulder, his arm almost useless. Though the wound needs attention Carr feels eyes upon him.

Casually retrieving his long-sword and not wanting to try jumping the fissure, Carr quietly continues east. Listening hard and hesitating over any noise, even sniffing the air, as he ambles along.

The giants unsure of what happened are still content with the day's entertainment. They decide to check things out in the morning light. Getting up the pair wander off unnoticed.

Walking along Carr wonders what happened. "Is someone watching over me? Did they have a deadly disease? Am I next?"

Passing by the spot where Tibor flattened him. "Oh good I don't have to even look for it." Carr observes the short-sword laying on a patch of stones.

Bending down he wipes the blade off, on his boot before sheathing it.

Climbing over patch of boulders the skies lighten, as Carr grows weary. Though higher up the mountain he's still along way from crossing the range.

Coming across a small, mossy clearing with a tiny spring running across it, Carr rests.

Carr gingerly takes off the pack, swords, armor, and shirt. The weight of the pack slowed blood-loss, but he's still lost much.

Tugging out a wrap from his full pack, he unrolls it.

Wanting to put the healing herbs on the wound they end up in the gapping wound. He almost passes out from seeing his own collarbone.

Wrapping the wound as best as possible he takes a drink and fills the canteen. Needing energy to continue Carr eats any bugs within the reach of his right arm.

Thinking of something his favorite cleric told him to do regularly but was thought a waste of time. With the warmth of the sun he leans against a boulder and closes his eyes trying meditation.

"Oh Violetta I wish you were here." He prays in hopes she'll hear. "I can't cauterize the wound until I get over the range to start a fire. Yes I did something bad but it was for Ma." He wonders with the blood that's lost if he can survive another three days. By that time, his arm will have to be removed.

With all that he's went through on little sleep, and the couple of pints of blood missing, the meditation becomes more than that, falling into a deep slumber.

A draft stirs him from a full sleep, cracking open an eye he focuses on the plant-life around him. Noticing the sun is low in the western sky.

Behind Carr a familiar voice growls in the old human language. "You break, promise made."

Heart pounding and eyes now open Carr turns his head slowly with a smile. "Sorry, great one, Men hunting me, my horse gone."

"Horse?" The lammasu asks. "Small, brown, leather saddle and bags?"

"Yes." Carr smiles. "That Bressi. Did you see her?"

Eyes showing signs of guilt, the lammasu struggles to reply. "I, am Sorry. Found horse tied to tree, wife and kids hungry…"

"No, no, no.." Carr is overrun with emotions.

Nodding slightly the lammasu sighs trying to apologize. "Very Sorry, I did not know. Mountain is covered in men. Figured it was theirs."

"Why? How… I had her seven years." Sad, frustrated and feeling defeat coming on Carr fights back tears. "Good horse, why? What about your goat? Eat Bressi bad. Just kill me now. I die here anyway."

Seeing Carr like a human child, the lammasu feels bad. "No need for that little man. Maybe I can help you? Some meat or..."

He hesitates not wanting to offer a special service that would be embarrassing to his kind and alike.

"No food." Carr releases a long sigh.

"I make you, one time only, promise…" The lammasu takes a deep breath, in disbelief of what he's about to offer the young human. "You must tell no one, ever, what I offer."

"Offer?" Carr listens to what he has to say.

"When the sun sets. I take you to town." Pointing behind them. "South, Ingleside, yes."

"Ingleside.?." Picturing Violetta, Carr hopes the creature is not messing with him softly asking. "You can get me to Ingleside?.. Really?.. How?"

Sighing the lammasu says. "I can, before dawn." In a stern tone he reminds Carr. "Yes. Never speak it. You keep promise."

A faint glimmer of hope returns to Carr. "You can get me to Ingleside, before dawn. O, can you really?"

Insulted by the question but proud to state. "Alone there and back in minutes."

Intrigued Carr answers. "Sure, if you can. You would save me. I would owe you great. I promise, I never met you."

"Good." Pointing at his chest. "I, Kryston, elder lammasu. Who you?"

Carr replies. "Kryston, I Carr, loyal rogue."

Raising a fuzzy brow at the title Kryston asks. "You are thief hmm. Life worth risking for shiny coins?" Pointing out his blood soaked wrap. "I smelt you all over. Easy to find."

Startled by the sight Carr reaches for his pack. "Rings worth it."

"Not dead in mountains." Noticing the heavy backpack, Kryston tests his character. "Much gold can not take you and gold." Knowing full well he can.

Carr freezes to ponder aloud. "Not much gold. Gems and jewelry." Showing a few of the bags inside. "I need off mountain more. Can I take some gems?"

Not surprised by his reply, Kryston asks. "Why?"

Speaking truthfully Carr explains digging out the last wrap. "Winter supplies." Pointing at the armor. "New suit, boots. Ma needs boots, some blankets."

For the first time in Kryston's twelve hundred seventy eight years, he's found a human he finds interesting. "Blankets? Kill animals, use furs."

Changing the shoulder dressing Carr, nods sharing his view. "Killed many as kid, not good for spirit. Like you only kill if needed. A ranger taught me much, fighting, survival and respect nature, it keeps us alive."

Impressed Kryston comments. "If your word true. Flying you to Ingleside good idea for both."

"Oh yes, truth." He answers slowly clueing in. "Fly? Fly to Ingleside?"

Kryston stretches out his wings smiling. "Yes, fly." Sitting back down he says. "At night. Many armed men on mountain. We wait for darkness. You tell me about your journey."

Glad to tell tales to anyone who'll listen Carr finishes the dressing while talking. Starting from the day he came home to find out the Lord Piate and his men had ransacked the farmhouse. Embellishing the story inside the city of Monsteil, while suiting up, he leaves out the fall from the window.

Enjoying the tale Kryston doesn't care if Carr's enhanced it, the diversion in life is welcomed.

As the sun finally sets they discuss what happened the night before. The lammasu shares his opinions on wights and specters but points to the short-sword suggesting the blade could be poisoned.

Both are unsure of the sword's markings and think its' best to treat the blade carefully.

Stretching out his body and wings Kryston yawns out. "You ready?"

"Yes." Answering unsure of what to expect Carr stands looking at his pack.

Catching him Kryston doesn't care having been entertained. "You can bring it."

A sly grin forms. "Yes, you sure?" It disappears as Carr pictures dropping down the mountain. "Can you still fly?"

Waving his paw aside Kryston replies. "We good, no worry."

"K-then." Utters Carr struggling to get it on with one arm.

Watching Kyston asks. "Your arm no good?"

Checking the arms ability Carr can grip and move the forearm with discomfort. The arm can't lift at the shoulder and pain shoots across his shoulder ever time he tries. "Need healer, one in Ingleside."

"Lucky for you." Now wondering if Carr will fall off in the air, Kryston points out. "You hang on tight, two hands. Or flat you be."

Getting the pack in place Carr says. "Yes, I will."

"Good." The lammasu informs. "You, sit on my shoulder, hold tight to mane. In air, you no move, just hold on."

Sliding the long-sword through the pack straps, Carr nods. "No worry I hold tight."

"Your life, you best." Crouching near Carr, Kryston points to his back hoping nobody is watching. "Climb on."

Carefully Carr sits on Kryston's shoulder grabbing up a couple long locks of the mane. "We good?"

The lammasu positions his body like a cat about to pounce, uttering. "Hold tight."

Springing up Kyrston leaps high into the air, Carr grips tighter then he realizes. Not affected Kryston beats his huge wings strongly flapping, climbing high into the evening sky.

Carr can't believe what he's feeling torn between fear and excitement.

He can see for thousands of leagues around except past Kyston's large head and flowing mane.

Cresting the peak Kryston has a little bit of fun with Carr diving sharply they sail down the mountainside at great speed.

Carr's butt lifts along with his stomach, teeth clenched and eyes shut, he's barely able to hold on.

Not wanting to lose the young rogue Kryston adjusts his wings gliding high.

Reseated Carr opens his eyes marveling at the nighttime view. What would have taken a day, takes only minutes. Clearing the range they soar south.

"You like, flying?" Kryston asks.

With eyes watering from the wind and heart pounding due to the height Carr replies. "Oh, yes."

Warning Carr and wanting to keep him quiet Kryston says. "Good, pray, nothing sees us. If attacked, I could drop you."

Now more nervous, Carr sits silently watching around. Picturing anything from archers to wyverns attacking them.

Unhindered hours pass and Carr relaxes listening to the beating wings and wind rushing by. Ahead a faint orange glow marks the town's location on the land.

Never viewing Ingleside from this vantage point Carr tries to identify each building as they distinguish themselves. Barely making out Violetta's place his ride comes to an end. The lammasu lands in a clearing just outside of town.

"Here you are." Kyrston says touching ground. "I dare not, go closer."

"This good." Carr gently slides off. "Thank-you."

The lammasu reminds him. "Just never tell."

Thinking nobody is going to believe him even if he did, Carr assures Kryston. "You spared and saved my life I owe you. If you need my help please ask. You know where I live, you come I will help."

About to tell him it's not necessary Kryston says. "Maybe one day I might, I will remember your promise. You have safe journey home."

"Okay." Carr steps back, to give the lammasu some room. "You fly safely home."

"Ahh, get home easy." Kryston winks, rubbing his fore paws together, growling strangely.

"What you say?" Asks Carr.

Winking once more Kryston vanishes from Carr's sight, magically teleporting himself home.

Carr stands wondering where he went. Looking towards the range debating if the beast even existed and if he'd ever see Kryston; the lammasu again.

"Geez, he's got to be a magic user." Carr speaks to no one. "The flying was great but if you could've just flashed me here, why not?"

Only the sound of rustling leaves is heard. Painfully shrugging it off Carr turns south happy to be so close to salvation.

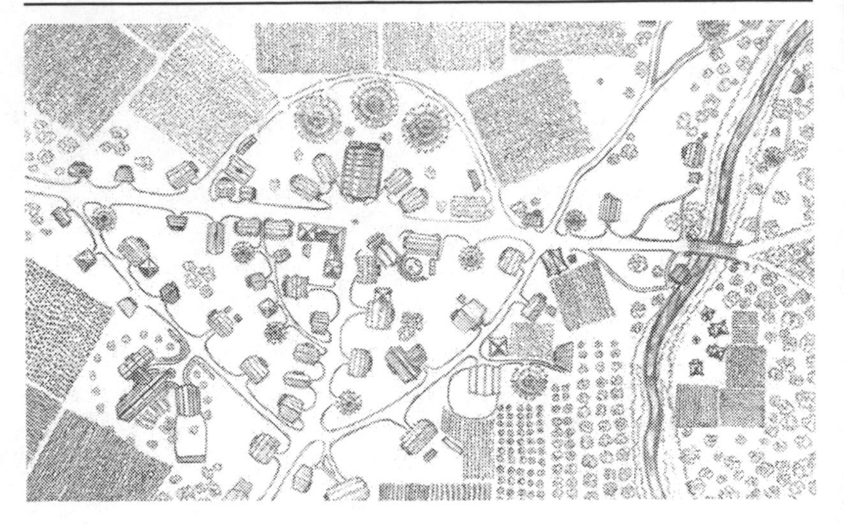

Cutting between Ingleside's outer fields Carr focuses on the centre of town.

"I can't wait to see Violetta. She's probably gonna kill me for showing up in the middle of the night… Then she'll resurrect me to bite off my head before healing me… Well at least I have coin, this time."

Between the elder's houses he walks into the centre of the dark, still town. Making his footsteps on the dirt seem loud. Attempting to cross quieter he tries to step lightly, only to falter scuffing the ground.

Taking the centre road south he can see Violetta's place an oil lamp burns in a window, letting people know she's there.

Approaching the old stone building Carr notices the straw roof needs repair. Taking a deep breath he knocks on the wooden door putting his best smile on.

The door opens, a tall women stands in the doorway. Her strong almost masculine hand is perched at the hip; not amused by his smile.

She looks him over. "I had a feeling you were going to show up. Tomorrow." Noticing his pale colour she calms but not enough for Carr to notice. "How bad is it this time?"

Playing tough Carr says. "It's just a scratch." Noting she looks angrier, with her red hair done up.

"Scratches don't require trips to a healer in the middle of the night." Shaking her head at him while stepping aside to allow him in. "Well lets have a look."

"Thank you Violetta." Carr speaks politely. "I am truly sorry for showing up so late. Again."

"Just get in here, fool." Violetta points out the all too familiar healing room. "You know what to do."

Carr enters a room in front of the main door. "I might need a hand with the armor."

Noticing the new glistening gash on the shoulder's covering. "How deep is it?"

Sitting on a heavy hardwood table, Carr sets his sword aside to attempt removing the backpack. "Ahh, it's deep. I saw bone."

Disappointed in Carr she forces herself not to slam any doors closing the front one. "What stupidity were you up to now?"

Standing in the room with a furled brow she watches him struggle with the pack, reading his emotions. "So you ripped somebody off and they caught up to you."

Knowing he can't lie to her, Carr sighs before answering. "Well kinda, but it was a good cause."

Hearing that angers her, Violetta speaks sternly. "There's no good reason to go get yourself killed. Just get that stuff off." She heads to the kitchen to gather some things, and cool down.

Knowing it's best not to speak, right now Carr contends quietly with his gear. Listening to her bang things around.

Returning with two large metal bowls and some clean rags, she passes barely glancing at him.

Setting a bowl of hot water and herbs on the table corner, the rags beside.

The second larger and empty bowl she places on the floor under the table.

Getting up Violetta watches Carr, obviously seriously wounded and nearing death's door.

"Here, let me help you." Violetta calms, taking the pack off the table. "I take it by the weight of this you can actually pay me. Or is it another statue."

Wincing Carr simply says. "No, I can pay you."

She helps remove his body armor. "I'm not taking any more stolen bric-a-brac." Setting the armor aside she sees the snuggly wrapped bandage is soaked with blood and there's a huge bruise on the left arm. "Did you fall out another window?"

Carr drops his head. "Ahh yah." The lack of blood keeps his face from blushing.

Unwrapping the bandage Violetta closes her eyes frustrated with the damage done. "Oh Carr, the herbs go on a wound not in it." Tossing the wrap aside. "How long ago did you get this wound?" She notices gangrene forming and the split muscle. "This is gonna be hard to heal."

Unsure of how much time has gone by he mumbles. "At least a day."

"Lay back." She assists and adjusts Carr on the table. "I'll need some other items, hold on a moment."

"Sure, thanks again Violetta." Carr watches her leave the room, wondering how bad is it.

After rummaging through an apothecary cabinet she returns hanging a medallion around her neck. Removing a vial from a pocket she hands it to Carr.

"Drink half." She sets up a chair beside Carr's head, positioning the floor bowl under the wound.

Carr does what she said, not liking the taste he comments. "Ee, tastes like moldy buns. What do you want me to do with the rest?"

"Hold it." She dips a rag into the water. "Hold it tight." Gently touching his head Violetta says in a soothing tone. "You'll live but this is going to hurt, a lot. Try not to move too much. You want something to bite down on?"

Carr remains calm. "No, go ahead." Studying her pretty face he gets lost in her emerald green eyes. "I have faith in you."

She almost smiles. "Try not to scream, people who work to live, are trying to sleep."

Taking the soaking rag she begins cleaning out the gapping shoulder wound. Carr's fists, toes and teeth clench, managing not to vocally cry out.

Carr comes close to passing out from pain. She stops flushing out the wound and gently wipes off the shoulder and table.

Wincing, Carr's shoulder throbs. "How bad is it?"

"Looks like a sharpened blade." Examining the wound more she states. "That'll give you got a better chance of healing. I can't promise full use of the arm."

Carr sighs and his speech slows. "I understand, but I do… appreciate you efforts."

Violetta knows he's about to go unconscious. "Carr pour the rest of the vial on your wound."

"O, kay." Carr does.

She takes the empty vial putting it in her pocket. "Now you can sleep if you want."

"I, am, o, kay." Carr tries to smile through the pain.

Seeing him helpless she strokes his head. "It's a good thing you and your mother are dear to me."

Rubbing her hands she clears random thoughts from her mind and focuses on the wound.

Beginning a chant she spreads out her fingers hovering over the wound to perform a lay-healing. The palms seem to glow as she glides them, hairs over the wound.

Repeating the calming chant she maneuvers the hands trying to close the wound. Absorbed by her voice Carr slowly losses consciousness.

Gradually the muscle tissue and veins stretch out reattaching, to pull themselves together. The bleeding subsides as the veins reconnect.

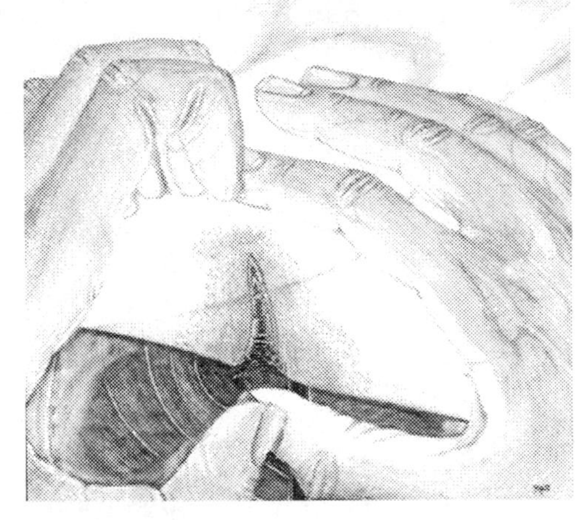

Hours of chanting go by before the lay-healing seals the wound, leaving no scar. Violetta takes a much, needed break.

Shaking out her arms and hands to disperse negative energy, she gets a thought of soldiers in the village searching buildings.

She grabs Carr's sword and body armor setting it outside the healing room.

Pulling the apothecary cabinet away from the wall she removes a nail from a support timber. Then pushes on the lower wall section opening it into a hidden room.

Assorted magical garments hang from the timbers. The floor is lined with bags, small chests, statues and carvings. She places Carr's gear inside, removing the rest of the scale armor as well.

On all the armor she finds brown animal hairs that she notes don't smell like horse.

Looking outside Violetta doesn't see Bressi or any other horse.

Curious to what the young thief has been up to she checks his pack before stowing it in the hidden room.

She examines every bag, sack and making her wonder, socks.

Violetta puts every thing back in the pack, except for a couple pieces of jewelry that caught her eye. Also keeping a dozen specific gems and fifty platinum coins for the healing.

Inspecting the powder she is uncertain of its nature. Not wanting Carr to have it, just in case, she places it in her cabinet. Thinking the next visit to the alchemist she'll have him identify the powder.

Violetta adds a small vial of healing potion, wrapped in a bandage to the pack; along with a pouch of healing herbs, in a second bandage.

Closing up and returning the cabinet, Violetta takes an ointment to Carr.

Sitting down she rubs the ointment over the shoulder. Chanting something a little different she gently massaging the entire shoulder.

Carr's breathing is very slow. Muscles so relaxed his body seems lifeless.

A rooster greeting the morning sun stops Violetta. Getting up she shakes out her arms and stretches the neck, popping a few spine bones back in place.

Taking a long look at Carr's necklace of protection and studying his spirit she goes to remove it. Noticing Carr's tiny necklace pouch she sees there's more than a coin in there.

Taking both off, she covers him with a blanket.

Closing the door and pocketing the medallion she exits the room.

Getting a bite to eat while brewing a tea she examines the contents of the tiny pouch.

Pulling the rings out she recognizes them, but can't place them. Two matching platinum rings, different only in size, simply engraved.

Reading an old rune inscription on the inside she remembers to whom the rings belong. Violetta's fingers wrap around them, looking towards Carr with a smile on her face.

Bringing them up to her chin with eyes welling up. "Ohh, Carr. You young fool. And carrying them over his heart." Hoping he's finally using his skills for the better, Violetta inserts them back into the pouch and hangs them around her own neck. Concealing them under her clothes.

Sitting down with legs crossed she sips the tea relaxing, thinking about what to do with Carr.

Setting the empty cup down she closes her eyes, clearing her mind to meditate.

"Bang, bang, bang."

Snapping to, hours later to some one pounding on the door, Violetta tries to focus. "Who is it?"

"Open up in the name of King Darvel."

Violetta rolls her eyes standing up uttering. "Come in quietly."

Carr wakes, listening motionless in the closed room as two of King Darvel's armed soldiers enter.

Spotting and remembering the healer the older and hairier of the men speaks to Violetta. "Good Woman we're searching for a thief who killed six of the King's men and stole his tax collections."

Sensing they don't really know who they're looking for, Violetta replies. "That's terrible who would dare kill and steal from the King?"

The second man starts opening the door to the healing room.

Violetta tries to distract them. "What does this scoundrel look like?"

"A young small human male with long black hair." States the older man

"Who's this then?" Asks the younger opening the door looking over Carr. "He matches the description."

Quickly she utters. "Hey let him be, he needs rest."

The older man steps back to look. "He does. What do you have to say?"

"Hey." She comes up behind them. "He staggered in around midnight last night. Gored by his own bull he walked here from his farm near the Cirran river."

The men pull back the blanket studying Carr, as he does an excellent job of faking sleep.

Noticing scratches to his hands and face many scars about his body, the younger man asks. "Where did he get gored then?"

Knowing all the marks on his body she replies. "It's the small red circle on the right side. Now let him be."

Both men look over his body not seeing it.

Pointing to Carr the young guard expresses his thoughts. "He's got plenty of scars and scratches that doesn't sound like a farmer."

The older man states his opinion. "What are you talking about man? One can get hurt pretty bad farming animals and working the land." He turns to Violleta. "I wanna believe you but he does look like the man we seek and some of the villagers said they saw him come this way last night."

Violetta asks. "When was the King robbed?"

"Three nights ago." The older man states.

Seeing Carr's freedom Violetta states a fact. "It takes three days to get here on horse back. He walked here last night. Collapsed on the table."

The younger man suggests. "He could've rode his horse to death and walked the rest of the way." His partner agrees with the logic.

Violetta points out. "Look how filthy he is, only those that labor hard get that dirty. The King's men took his horses as tax payment forcing him to walk here. With no coin I had to heal him for free."

Carr listens to her and can't believe the lies she's spinning. The men are thinking it over.

The younger man reminds his partner. " Didn't the Captain tell us to bring back, anybody that comes close to the description?"

"Oh, great." Violetta goes on. "So he barely makes it here due to the King's men. I waste my energy to save him, for free. And now the King's men are going to cart him off. Most likely to his doom just because he's got long black hair."

"Easy, Mam." The older male tries to calm her.

She continues. "You know, no matter what he'll say to defend himself, he'll be accused of lying and jailed. Why don't you just kill him while he sleeps."

Surprised by her words the men aren't sure what too say and look at each other. Carr's wondering if they'll stab him where he lays.

The older man speaks in an annoyingly calm manner. "Now easy there, good women. I trust your character after all you are a cleric." Turning to his companion he explains. "This good natured healer's only concerns are the suffering of others."

"That's right." Comments Violetta.

"...Mam your reputation of a healer is known throughout the continent." The man continues. "You also turned down King Darvel's request to be his personal healer."

Violetta grins. "I remember that day. He was so offended that someone would dare say no to him." She recovers Carr.

The younger man looks at her strangely. "You said no? To the King?"

Violetta rolls her eyes at the young man's naivety. "It's like I told your King. Every being has a right to live. My oath is to make sure to ease the suffering of others, not to become wealthy from it. I'm certainly not interested in wiping the runny noses of the rich and powerful."

"Ahh, don't worry about him." The older man adds. " The King did find a competent cleric but he's not as attractive as yourself nor as voiced."

Violetta pastes a smile on. "Oh thank you for the kind words good sir."

The younger man asks. "Shouldn't we get the Captain's opinion?"

"If she's not going to help a King I don't think she'd help a common thief." The older man points out. "But check around for any armor, weapons or bags of gold around." Turning to Violetta. "Your okay with that?"

She doesn't have any real choice. "Go ahead." Not worrying about them finding anything, as it's hid.

The older man steps closer to Violetta. "I believe you. If he finds nothing we'll just leave you in peace."

The younger man searches Violetta's bedroom. Carr's hoping that his stuff is concealed, especially the short-sword and pack.

Still wanting to talk with Violetta the man says. "I am sorry for disturbing you." He escorts her out of the room closing the door. "I also want to thank you."

Curious Violetta asks. "A thank you? For what?"

He explains. "I few years ago you saved a young boy, from the northern village of Tess. He was run down by a raiding party."

She only has to think but a second. "Oh yes. I remember the poor boy and that poor village. So many needlessly died there. He had so many broken bones. How is he?"

"To watch him you'd never know, he suffered so." The man points proudly to his chest. "That's my great nephew, Mathewe. He's strong and fast and will lead a long good life, thanks to you."

With a genuine smile she replies. "I'm glad to have helped and it's wonderful news to hear he's doing well. Of course you're welcome."

The other man exits the bedroom shaking his head no, while passing his partner to check the open kitchen and sitting room.

Carr remembers the trip north that year with Violetta and Hal. They went to help, finding the village nearly wiped out. He was the one who found the mangled boy while looking for valuables to take. Instead of helping the villagers, they had to build a huge funeral pyre, a very sad and sobering journey.

Violetta tries not to watch the man search her stuff, suggesting to them. "If it's a thief you're after, why not try the guild to the north."

The older man nods. "The King thinks so too, he's dispatched his best company of horsemen there. We're to split up if we don't find him here. Soldiers are scouring the mountain range and another group was sent to Lafhee. Some of us will take the road to Lahfee. Two are already taking the road to the Cirran River. The rest headed to Ahn."

"There's nothing here." The young man states.

"Let's go." The older man smiles at Violetta. "Sorry for the intrusion ma,am. We appreciate your help."

Violetta shows them the front door. "I understand your just following orders." Opening it for them. "May your duties go safely. So you may return to help Mathewe become a man."

Exiting they simply say. "Take care."

She watches them cross the dirt street to bother other villagers, mumbling. "Ma,am. Insulting. Disrespectful mindless bafoons." Violetta returns inside focused on the healing room.

Carr hears the front door close; peeking to see he's alone in the room he opens his eyes. Violetta pushes open the door and quickly approaches Carr.

Cuffing him upside his head she speaks in a low stern voice. "Alright fool, an explanation. You stole all the King's taxes and killed his men? Keep in mind I saved your skin, twice, today."

Carr rubs his head. "Hey, you don't have to hit me. Even though I deserve it.""

"Alright..." Violeta slyly grins. "...speak the truth and I won't infect your little fuzzy nuts with some awfully itchy disease."

"Okay, okay. That won't be needed." Carr sits up hanging his legs off the table. "Violetta I always appreciate what you do for me. I thank you, greatly. If it wasn't for your blessed hands I'd be dead a dozen times by now."

She grumbles. "At least a dozen." Reading his emotions he's being genuine.

Carr explains his side. "Yes I did break into the tax collection building and steal. I'm sure you had a look at all I took. I can't carry much more than that. It's that Lord Piate, the tax collector, he's stealing from the King. I found a chest in the man's bedchamber, full of treasure. I'm sure the King isn't unaware of.

Piate's probably using me as a scapegoat keeping the tax collected for himself."

Violetta calms slightly. "I believe you for two reasons. I met that Lord Piate. I would never trust that slob of an excuse for a man. I also know you work alone and couldn't steal all that's collected, without the help of magic."

Carr says. "You forgot one other reason."

"Yah?" Violetta looks him over "What's that?"

He smugly smiles noting. "You were reading my mind as I spoke."

Astonished, touched and a little offended by his true accusation, she sways the conversation. "What the hell's wrong with you? Going after a King's treasure. Rightly or wrongly collected your just asking for trouble. Why didn't you j.."

Frustrated she changes the subject. "Just take the bed in the loft. You'll need plenty of rest. Before you leave in the morning." She helps him off the table.

"Sure thing Violetta." Carr swallows raising the courage to ask. "Ahh, can I ask another favor?"

She loudly exhales. "What is it?"

He asks softly. "Can you find me a new horse?"

"A new horse?" She looks into his eyes. "What happened to Bressi?"

Sighing Carr answers her. "I kinda traded her for a ride to town."

Sensing sadness washing over Carr she asks. "You What?" Looking at him with disbelief. "You loved that horse, and you traded her for a ride into town?"

Staring into his welling eyes Violetta figures something happened out there. "You get stranger and stranger." Guiding him out of the room. "But I guess I can go see."

Thinking of what must of happened to Bressi Carr fights back a tear thanking Violetta.

Opening up the hidden room she guides him. Carr ducks in, making his way back to a vertical ladder fixed to the end wall, leading to the loft.

Shakily climbing the ladder Carr tells Violetta. "Take some coins out of my pack to pay for the horses and everything."

"I will." Violetta replies bending down to the pack watching Carr scale the ladder. "You try and get some more sleep. When I return I'll fix us an early supper." Mumbling to herself. "I'll need to sleep early tonight."

"Thanks again Violetta." Carr carefully steps onto the upper floor, lit by small round windows on either side of the vertical walls.

Violetta counts out fifty gold and an extra ten platinum. While Carr makes himself comfortable, more weak then tired.

Closing up the hidden room she speaks softly. "Rest up Carr, I'll be back in awhile."

"I'll be here." He whispers back.

Taking an apple with her to snack on she leaves, for the village stable.

The two soldiers who searched her place are starting their way up the curved street to the west.

Cutting behind her home she walks east saying polite hellos to her neighbors.

A teen male is dumping a bucket of water into an almost empty watering trough, inside the stable pen.

She calls to him. "Excuse me young man, are there any horse's for sale here?"

Barely looking at her, he shakes his head no. "Mr. Tavistock has several newly trained horses."

"Thank you." Violetta smiles enjoying the warm day and fresh air, continuing north up the curved street greeting the other villagers as she passes them.

Crossing the main road she stops at a small round hut to see how one of Ingleside's newest citizens is doing. After sharing some ooos and ahhs, with the family and a little dietary advice, she proceeds up a smaller northern road.

Ahead she can see Mr. Tavistock leading a small herd of horses, from a field into a pen off his barn.

Walking up the path to the farm Violetta calls out to him. "Good day, Mr. Tavistock."

The man finishes latching the pen gate, looking up to see her approach. "Well, good day to you Violetta."

The thickly built man, of early elder years, smiles walking to the other side of the pen. "What brings you out here, today? The cool breeze?"

She watches the different horses and their movements attempting to find a suitable choice, spotting an all black mare. "The stable-boy says you've some newly trained horses.

As she leans against the fencing of the pen a chestnut coloured horse nudges her shoulder. "Oh hello." Violletta checks over the horse.

"Aye." Replies Mr. Tavistock leaning on the fence beside her, pointing to the animals. "Best group I've ever trained. "

Violetta strokes the chestnut horse. "They seem well. Which ones are the most responsive?"

He watches her with the horse. "What do you need it for? Just riding or hauling?"

"Riding but It's not for me. It's gotta be able to learn new things quickly." Violetta has a look in the horse's mouth. "Although this chestnut one seems like an excellent choice."

The man nods informing her. "He does seem to take to you. But if its' for someone else I'd say the brown colt with the white socks, or the black mare"

Patting the horse she asks. "Is there something wrong with this one?"

"No." Mr. Tavistock suggests. "He just doesn't take to most. He must sense your good nature."

Violetta senses strong emotion coming from the stallion. "I get the feeling if he was human I'd have a suitor at my door."

Chuckling at the idea Mr. Tavistock leans in winking. "Girl, every single man in town wants to court you including a few of us married ones."

Violetta smiles at the thought. "Your sweet Gerald." Watching the black mare. "Have you a saddle and gear for sale also?"

"Aye, there's a old set, in decent shape in the barn." He looks to see what she's got her eye on. "The black one is a good horse almost doesn't need a rider. Who's it for? Or should I ask?"

She utters softly. "I think you know."

He whispers back. "Our young thief, eh? Well that would be an excellent choice for him."

Seeing someone different on the property, Mr. Tavistock's youngest boy, of ten years, runs out to investigate.

"How much for the horse and saddle?" Violetta inquires, watching the boy approach.

Mr.Tavistock makes a generous offer. "For you fifty gold and I'll give you the chestnut horse, for saving my baby girl last winter."

Violetta looks him in the eye. "That's more than fair, but I'll gladly pay you for such a fine animal."

The boy stands on a lower fence rail.

"Ahh," Mr. Tavistock sees a perfect match between owner and animal. "You can't put a price on a child's life. You go ahead and take him. Besides I'll have a hard time finding another he'll take to. He'll end up pulling a wagon or getting whipped for not responding to someone he don't like."

The boy asks. "What horse Pa?"

He looks down at his boy. "She's taking the black mare and the chestnut one."

"Good." The boy speaks his mind. "I don't like that one, it tries to bite me."

Chuckling Mr. Tavistock says to Violetta. "See that, the horse is picking you." Turning the boy. "John do your old man a favor and saddle up the black mare."

"Okay Pa." The boy jumps down, hesitating to ask. "Ah which saddle Pa?"

"The one you're always playing on." He shoos the boy away.

Violetta reaches for the coins in her pocket. "What do you want platinum or gold?"

"Oh a choice, eh?" Mr. Tavistock watches her. "Best make it gold."

"Alright." She separates the coins handing him the gold as she finds them.

Watching John take the horse inside the barn Mr. Tavistock asks Violetta. "So how much of what Darvel's men are saying is true."

Violetta was waiting for someone to ask. "He stole back some rings. But did kill a couple men."

Tavistock tells her what he was told. "The men that came here said he stole the King's whole tax collections for the year, and killed several men." He laughs a little. "The boy's got balls, but I wanted to know. How one small boy can carry twenty times his weight?" He smiles. "Just like his father. Eh?""

Violetta states what Carr suggested. "Piate may have used the foolish stunt for his own benefit."

"Oh yeah. I can see that." Mr. Tavistock finishes her thought. "Take the collection for himself, blame a thief. Kill any men who don't see the story his way. Convenient, I wonder how much Darvel would pay for such treasonous information."

"Yes, I can see it like that too." Violetta hands him the last of the gold. "Are you sure I can't pay you. Healing children is always charitable."

He shakes his head no. "Forget it. Besides I'd rather give you those horses, than let Darvel's men take them. Even worse, haggling with those thieves, from the guild. Not to mention you do so much for the townsfolk. And that young thief gives us men something to talk about."

She raises a brow of concern at the need men have for foolish and violent tales. "Us women talk about him too. And how glad that you men don't take part in such a disregard for your lives and our feelings."

He laughs at the truth. "Anymore, for some of us." Remembering his past.

Wishing to change the subject Violetta says. "If you're sure, I'll take him. He seems like a good animal. I haven't ridden in a year."

"You sure can." He reminds her. "I've only one saddle to sell."

She boldly states. "I prefer bareback anyway." She climbs the fence to sit on the horse.

He raises his brow and forms a grin. "Oh, really." Moving over to steady the horse.

Violetta adjusts her position, barely having to coax the animal, the horse trots proudly around.

Tavistock finds the sight amusing. "See I told you, he picked his owner. He looks happy to have you on him." Watching Violetta's body bounce with the horses', softly mumbling. "I'd be happy too."

The boy comes out of the stable leading the mare. "Here she is Pa." Handing him the reins.

Wanting to watch Violetta a little longer he says "Thanks boy. Hey go ask your mom if she wants anything from town."

Excited John asks loudly "Can I go too?"

Gerald replies. "Aye. But only you."

"All right!" Exclaims John, kicking up dust tearing back to the farmhouse.

Amused by the boy Violetta comments to Gerald. "Betcha' he's going to be a handsome strapping man someday. Is he much help around the farm?"

"Aye." Tavistock jokes with her. "Of late, he took over for the rooster."

Unsure how to respond she asks. "How's that?"

"Oh." He laughs lightly telling her. "He's been obsessed with monsters of late. And late at night he wakes the whole house, pointing to shadows in the dark. Last night it was a griffon." Pointing to the woods north of the farm. "With a rider. I've never seen one, close up. He's certainly never seen one."

Now thinking hard on what Carr said, she turns to him. The horse automatically stops beside Tavistock, Violetta pats the horse, asking. "A griffon? With a rider, you say?"

"Aye. Kids eh?" More impressed with her and the horse he queries. "Are you actually guiding him?"

"I'm not sure he's doing what I want him too." She informs him, still curious about the griffon.

"I tell you lass." Mr. Tavistock shares his view. "It takes years for a good horse to respond to its' rider like that. Most never will. This horse and you are a perfect match."

Agreeing with him, she says. "I think I will keep him. And they do keep I stall open for me at the stable. Yes, why not."

Happy to see a perfectly suited pair, he suggests. "I do have a lead I can let you have."

"Yes, a good idea." She smiles down at him.

The smile gives him some lift. "I'll fetch you one." Heading into the barn.

Stroking the horse's neck and mane, she inquires. "So what time of night did he wake you?"

Returning from the barn he displays the leather lead. "Here we are." Approaching the horse to tie the lead around its neck. "Hmm, I'm not sure when. Maybe after midnight." Gerald clues in looking up to Violetta. "Was it our young thief?"

"Maybe." Hesitating Violetta looks around for prying eyes. "He said he traded his horse for a ride into town."

Making sure the lead is secure he ponders the statement. "He had that little tan mix right?"

"Yes." She tells him. "He had her seven years? Loved that horse."

Gerald hands her the end of the lead. "Trading your horse for a ride on a griffon?"

They both wonder quietly, as John exits the farmhouse running back. One by one his four other siblings stand outside the farmhouse door noticeably disappointed they didn't get to go.

Making the first comment Mr. Tavistock points out. "I was told the only one who can ride a griffon is one who's been there since it hatched. Or however they come to be. In the wild they're supposed to be very dangerous. Is he that smooth of a talker?"

Violetta jests with him. "Like a baby's bottom complete with the occasional stinky mess."

He laughs out loud, as John opens the pen gate. "What's so funny?"

Not wanting to say too much Violetta inquires. "Your father tells me you saw a griffon and a rider last night. Is it true?"

Figuring he's being made fun of, John scowls at his dad. "I did see it."

"Easy boy." Chuckles Gerald leading the two horses out.

Violetta asks. "So tell me John, how do you know it was a griffon?"

Latching the gate John explains. "Well it had really, really big wings. It had four legs. And ahhh it was huuuge. The rider looked like a little kid on its back."

Gerald lifts his boy onto the mare joking. "Just like you on this horse."

Not amused John tries to ignore his father. "At first I thought it was a pegussis, but it didn't have a horse's head."

Gerald climbs on the saddle behind his son, asking Violetta. "What do you think of that?"

Violetta responds with. "I wish I had been able to see it for myself."

Nudging the black mare Mr. Tavistock gets the animals moving towards the town adding. "Being hunted by many. A hungry beast willing to trade for a ride. I suppose it could happen."

Looking at the both of them John asks. "What are you talking about?"

Violetta changes the subject. They discuss a list of things Mrs. Tavistock wants from town.

Entering the village they greet and wave to their fellow citizens as they pass.

Reaching the stable they're told the soldiers have left. Unknown to the villagers two of Darvel's men remained in hiding to watch the town.

Parting company they wish each other well. One of her favorite ways to remember a man, spending time with children, she watches them wander off.

After paying the stable-boy a platinum coin she instructs him to tend to the horses and to make sure the mare is ready by morning to travel. For a gold he'd roll in a pigpen, gladly accepting the request.

With thoughts and questions for Carr, when he wakes, she returns home to prepare a much needed, nutritional meal.

Eventually the heavenly aroma of a hot meal drifts into the loft causing Carr to stir. He tests his arm and shoulder, extremely weak, but moving as they should.

As his feet hit the floorboards with a creak, Violetta knows its time to open the hidden room, returning to set out the meal.

Driven by smell and a grumbling belly Carr hastily climbs down the ladder. Missing the last rung he hits ground unexpectedly. No worse for wear and still upright, he carefully exits the room.

Attempting to be sweet Carr utters. "Other then you. What smells sooo good?"

Violetta can't wait to grill him, but tries to restrain herself. "I prepared a vegetable stew, spiced just right."

Smiling Carr rubs his empty belly. "Mmm, nice and spicy hot."

"Well not to hot, you're still healing." Violetta displays one of her special loaves of bread. "I had a little bit of cinnamon left." Picking up a pitcher she pours out two cups of water. "Come, sit down before you fall down."

Not sure if she's just being friendly or up to something, Carr keeps an eye on her taking a seat at the wooden table. "Cinnamon bread eh?"

"It's been awhile for me too." Violetta takes a large ladle and scoops out two bowls full of stew from a steaming pot hung in the fireplace. "I made sure to include things that will help your healing."

"Thanks Violetta, for always taking such good care of me." Thirsty he drinks down the cup of water and pours up another.

"You're quite welcome Carr." She sets the bowls on the table, sitting down. "I can't leave your mother to fend for herself."

Thinking that's the reason she's being nice Carr says. "Yah, I got to get back soon there's still a couple fields to be cut down."

Wondering how to direct the conversation Violetta responds. "Yes that would be a good idea." She takes a knife and slices up the loaf. "It makes me happy to see you, still taking care of her."

Blowing on a spoonful of stew Carr looks over inquiring. "What about you don't you want some one to look after you?"

Knowing he's referring to himself she says. "I haven't needed a man yet. How's your friend Sonja?"

"As pretty as ever. But nowhere near the woman you are." He smiles at her trying to be smooth.

She smiles back. "Well you're still too young, for me to take seriously."

Purposely sighing loudly, he says. "I guess it's always going to be the same between us."

"I think you're just taken by me because I've saved you so many times." She does appreciate the attention, adding what he hates hearing. "If you weren't always trying to run off chasing gold and trinkets…"

"I know if I was only happy to be a farmer." Discouraged by the ongoing argument Carr restates his view. "But it's so dull, stuck on the farm."

Violetta pulls the tiny pouch out. "Is this what you risked your skin for?" Taking it off she hands it back over to Carr.

Hanging the pouch around his neck. "Yeah, it is." Not sure how she actually feels about it.

A big warm smile covers her face. "That is the only one, of your foolish quests I can appreciate."

"Yah?" Carr looks at her strangely. "I didn't think you'd approve."

"Killing people over them. No." Violetta points out. "Your father would've been behind you. I have a feeling your mother is not going to like the idea. I'm sure she'll like the gesture. Did you at least tell her where you were going?"

Softly Carr responds. "Ah, no."

She shakes her head at him. "That's disrespectful to make your mother worry."

"Well er ahh…" Carr tries to defend his actions. "I said I wanted to get them back for her. But she said it wasn't worth risking my life over."

"Well Carr I feel the same way." Violetta remains calm explaining. "Sure they've got a sentimental value but they are just fashioned pieces of metal."

Carr nods at the truth. "I couldn't let them end up in some King's treasure house never to be seen again."

Seeing an opportunity to find out what else he's been up to she asks. "You risked life and limb for those trinkets, yet traded your horse for a ride into town. Can you explain that to me?" Taking in a mouthful of stew studying Carr's emotional response.

His eyes become distant as he struggles to carefully answer her question. "I promised I wouldn't talk about it. Let's just say. I didn't mean to trade her for a ride. I had no choice."

Sensing truth and sadness she inquires. "Why didn't you have a choice?"

Sighing again Carr answers. "I knew my wound was bad and if I didn't make it to you. I would have died out there."

Agreeing with his statement she nods. "Yes you didn't have much time left." Knowing he keeps a promised word she bluffs a statement. "Last night you were seen, flying on the back of a griffon. Dropping you off outside of town."

Carr's eyes widen, as he quickly answers her. "I promised I would discuss it. The griffon threatened to hunt me down, or Ma, if anyone found out."

Satisfied with his response she inquires. "Is Bressi really gone?"

Carr stops eating, "Yes."

Feeling bad for making Carr sad and wanting him to continue to eat she reluctantly inquires. "Well tell me about your journey and you don't have to tell me anything further about the griffon." Hoping his story telling will alter his mood.

It slowly does, by the time he gets to the ogre his appetite returns. She also informs him the medallion may be a curse to him as well.

He leaves out the first encounter with Kryston. Mainly describing the path he took over the mountains. Violetta doesn't recall such a path but prefers to stay to the main routes when traveling.

Inside the city Carr boasts to Violetta that the mystery innkeeper wanted him. She doesn't believe him but remains quiet.

As he goes into detail on the Lord's bedchamber Violetta pours out a second bowl of stew. The rest of the tale up to fleeing the city and the fight in the range stays the same.

The last part of the mountain tale he only says the basics. The griffon found him and wanted him out of the area. When Carr told the beast he my not make it because his horse was gone the griffon felt bad for eating Bressi and offered to fly him to Ingleside.

Violetta doesn't believe the griffon story but knows Carr made a promise not to talk about it so she doesn't ask. She does easily get Carr to describe the flight. He gladly does going into great detail.

By the time he reached Violetta's the pair managed to eat the loaf of bread and Carr got three bowls of stew into his stomach.

Rubbing his bloated belly Carr compliments her. "That was mighty tasty stew Violetta. Is there anything you can't do?"

Cleaning up she replies. "Yeah, I can't keep people from killing each other or themselves."

Carr yawns stretching out his body. "Hey? Did you put galenous in the stew?"

Grinning she answers. "Yup. I wanted to make sure you got some more sleep in."

"Oh.." Carr looks around his eyes get heavy. "And I ate three bowls. Didn't I get enough sleep already?"

Snickering at him she points up. "Yah and if you don't want to wake up on the floor you best return to the loft."

Carr reluctantly agrees and she helps him back into the hidden room.

Making certain he doesn't wipe out, she follows him up the ladder and even tucks him in.

Saying their goodnights Violetta, requiring a long sleep herself, heads for her room.

The next morning Violetta fixes a basic meal of fruit and bread. Filling Carr's canteen with water and making sure he's got food for the ride home.

Recovering from the galenous Carr wakes descending to the main floor.

Sitting at the table he notices his gear is assembled.

"Good morning Carr." In a great mood Violetta greets him. "I trust you slept through the night?"

Smiling back Carr says. "I should've after you drugged me. But I still love you."

She laughs informing him. "I had some too."

"I see you're happy to get rid of me this morning." He jests pouring up a drink of water.

Passing by him she kisses him on the forehead. "It's almost noon. I slept well too."

She hasn't kissed him since he was a little boy. Carr gives her the once over. "I don't think I've seen you this happy." Starting to place his armor back on. "That is you, isn't it?"

"Yah" She snickers. "It has been awhile." Helping him tie up the coverings she says. "Yesterday I got you a new horse it's at the stable."

"Really?" Looking her in the eye Carr states. "You're the best Violetta someday you'll have to let me make it up to you."

Already with an idea she tells him. "Take care of your mother. That would please me."

"Of course." Not satisfied with her request he inquires. "Come on now you do so much for me. I must be able to do something for you?"

"Okay, since your asking." She lets him know. "Stay on the farm, find a nice girl to marry, raise a family and stop risking your life foolishly."

He shakes his head. "I should have figured. There's nothing you want?"

She has the perfect answer. "Sure there is."

Frustrated but curious he inquires. "What is it?"

A sly grin forms as she answers him. "Let me do the marrying and help with the birthing."

"You are something." Giving up for now he asks. "So what kind of horse did you get?" Picking up a peach he takes a big bite out of it.

"A mare." Not knowing the breeds she says. "She's a little bigger then Bressi. And I'm sure you'll like her colouring."

"Oh yah?" Swallowing he guesses. "Is it white with brown spots."

"No."

Not really caring, as he trusts her decisions. "Well you picked it that's all that matters and at least I don't have to walk home."

Violetta says. "I have a new horse too."

Trying to recall if she ever had one. "Oh yah.?"

"Yes." She replies actually wanting to go for a ride. "He's a beautiful chestnut colour with dark brown mane and tail."

He pulls his boots on to finish suiting up with the shin guards. "I can't remember seeing you with a horse of your own."

Thinking back she says. "It has been a long time. About a decade."

"Um, Violetta." Wishing to ask another favor. "I don't suppose you have a vial or two of healing potion? I can pay you."

Pondering over it briefly, she knows he'll end up needing a second. "Well I already put one in your pack, but you, you will do something foolish." Opening a cabinet door she pushes some bottles aside. "I think a can spare one. And next time use it for a wound like this one." Tapping his left shoulder.

"Okay but I can, pay you." Offers Carr knotting up the last strap.

Rolling the vial in a bandage Violetta declines. "Just take it and for heavens sake stay out of trouble."

"I'll try." Strapping the short-sword on he asks. "Did you look at this blade?"

Inserting the vial into the pack she glances at the sword. "Yes its nice."

"No." Carr queries. "Do you think the blade is poisonous?"

She stands carefully drawing the sword. "Well the handle feels very negative, its taken lives." She turns it over reading the ruins inscribed on the blade. "Not good." Cautiously she returns the blade and goes back to the cabinet.

"What?" Carr watches her. "Is it poisonous?"

"Yes." Finding a different vial, Violetta wraps it right away. "It a venomous blade alright."

Carr is happy but knows not to show it around the present company. "I best, be careful with it."

Knowing she can't tell him to get rid of it, she replies. "No. You best hide that somewhere. You wouldn't want your Ma to find it accidentally."

Not thinking ahead Carr utters. "Oh, yeah."

"Yah." Violetta turns to him showing the bundled vial. "This is anti-poison. Try to keep it out of the sunlight, it'll ruin the potion." Stuffing it into the pack.

Carr appreciates her kind heart. "Thank you so much Violetta. To honor your generosity I'll stash the sword when I get home and forget about it."

Liking the first part of the statement, she knows he won't be able to forget about it. "Yes, please hide it well enough, you forget where it is." She helps him get his pack on.

"I will." Carr makes an invitation. "You should come down, before the winter and we'll put you up for the night. I'm sure Ma would like you to stop in."

Picking up the long-sword she accepts. "Yes I should. With a new horse. A nice ride. Maybe late next month." She notices the numerous nicks taken out of the blade. "I don't like people to have these things, but you should invest in a new weapon."

He takes the sword recalling how each nick came to be. "It's getting dull too." Sliding it between his back and pack, jokingly asking for her opinion. "Have any suggestions on a new blade?"

Her suggestion is half humor and mainly truth. "Something useful. Like a, new sickle. They, can kill."

Eyes rolling, Carr replies smartly. "They do have an advantage. I prefer a little distance from my foe."

Opening the front door Violetta steps out into the warm cloudy day. "Come fool, lets get you moving. You aren't gonna make Ahn before dark."

Following, Carr shields his eyes. "Oh the sun…I'll make the campsite though."

She looks at him and laughs once. "I can't wait for the day that old, if you can call it a bridge, collapses and you end up in the Grun"

Enjoying a good creaky crossing Carr says. "I kinda like it. It's like gambling. Will he make it across or will he be swimming."

"Drowning you mean." Poking his backpack. "Not to mention you'll be crossing it in the dark."

"Ahh, I've got a new horse to try out." He grins.

She warns him. "Come on now, don't run her into the ground."

Wrapping his arms around her. "Thanks again."

She likes it, but plays different patting him on the back and breaking the hold. "Next time try and make it social and not late."

Nodding Carr grins. "I'll try and I'll try to behave." He starts to walk away. "Besides I'm only gonna take the rest of the fields down and a trip across the swamp for winter supplies. This was probably my last job."

Older and seasoned she knows better. "It's not good to lie to yourself like that. You're stuck on the same road as trouble. Look for an alternate path."

Hesitating at the corner of her place he glances back. "Hey trouble's a good friend of mine." Waving bye he rounds the corner.

Violetta sighs knowing from his lifeline, worse suffering will come before he learns. She mentally wishes him well and will say a few prayers for him. For now she returns inside to cleanse the house of negative energy.

Strolling over to the stable his eyes finally adjust to the daylight. Some of the locals take notice of him whispering to each other. He doesn't mind at all and walks tall.

The waiting stable-boy sees him coming and knows for certain who the horse is for and fetches the mare from the stall.

Carr walks up to the stable scanning the area, spotting the similarly aged male retrieving a saddled horse. "Excuse me. I'm Carr. Did Violetta tell you I have a horse here? I see your busy just point out the stall and I'll get her myself." Watching the guy lead out a beautiful, all black horse.

"Yup" The stable-boy replies. "I saw you coming and knew this was your horse." Pointing to the black scale, handing over the reins.

"No way.?!" Carr takes a good look at her. "Wow, she picked out a beauty."

Agreeing the guy informs Carr. "Oh yes, the soldiers were talking about this one. And a couple of the others in town were saving their coin to purchase her." He grins. "They're mad. One was only a couple gold away."

Carr looks at him. "Wasn't you was it?"

Shaking his head no. "I've got a good one."

"Oh well then." Carr shrugs before hoisting himself in the saddle.

Holding the mare steady the stable-boy inquires. "What did you pay for her?"

Unsure Carr answers, trying to impress him with a wink. "I don't know. Violetta bought her for me."

That comment removes a smile from the stable-boy's face; Jealous of Carr's position with the towns' favorite woman. "She bought her for you?"

Knowing, that information will quickly circulate around the small village. "Oh yah." To put the stable-boy at ease and add to the gossip he says. "But that's what family is for."

Relieved that Carr's not a threat for Violetta's affection, the boy utters. "Oh sure."

Nudging the horse to leave the barn, Carr waves once. "Thanks for having her ready. Take care."

"Sure, have a good ride." The stable-boy waves slightly; looking for someone to update, on the village's exciting week.

Showing off Carr gets the horse to gallop across the grass. Tearing by Violetta's Carr calls out as they pass. "Thank you! Good woman. She's great! See you next time."

She hears him and the horse go by, looking to the heavens reassuring herself. "The boy just needs guidance. Send him a smart, strong, young woman."

Tearing between the houses Carr cuts across the grassy field for the western road to Lafhee.

Keeping their distance the villagers speculate on what's happened and will happen to Carr and them.

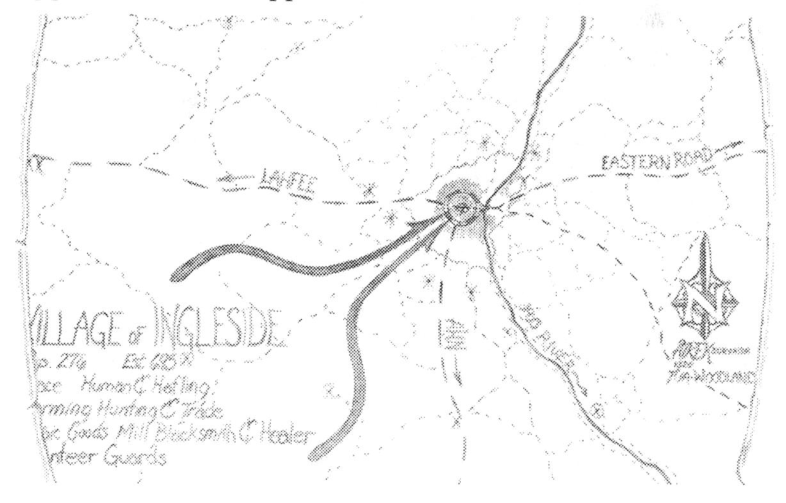

Carefree and thrilled with the horse Carr enjoys the moment. Following the rhythm of the racing black mare he focuses on the road before him. Completely missing the two remaining soldiers watching him in a small clearing outside of town.

Immediately as Carr gallops past they retrieve their horses to give chase.

Never to look back Carr is fortunate to have a younger and faster horse, as they easily escape the soldier's view.

Winding their way through the tree covered road both happy to be running wild.

After several leagues he slows the horse up for its own good. To also find a nearing path that'll lead him to the campsite north of Ahn.

Way too far behind the pursuing soldiers will never see him take the trail.

Entering the path, a tall weed's branch breaks pointing the direction went.

Comforted by Violetta and being so close to home Carr never bothers to look back. Instead they leisurely navigate the old forest path, as Carr thinks of what to call the new horse. Chuckling at the common, unsuited names. Shaking his head to the obscure lengthy titles. Eventually they reach the river crossing.

The sinking sun still illuminates the riverbed. An old primitively constructed bridge rests atop the high riverbank.

Getting down Carr leads the horse to the bridge. Made up of four strapped together delimbed trees.

Not knowing how long it has been there he heeds Violetta's warning. Allowing the horse to carry the heavy pack.

Only a few steps on the bridge and Carr is forced to stop it seems the horse is reluctant.

Gently tugging the animal while talking sweet, gets her started.

Out over the river the horse's legs tremble and the timbers creak.

Looking down at the river for fish Carr notices the bridge is starting to sag. Making a longer stride crossing the middle, the horse decides it's time to get off when a loud crack rings out.

Knocking Carr aside the horse quickly clears the rickety bridge.

Carr drops managing to dig fingertips into the old wood, holding on. The fall to water isn't far or too deep he'd just prefer to stay dry.

Looking at the horse with annoyance he curses. Pulling himself up and rolling onto the timbers, the horse finds a way down to the river to drink.

Sitting up he notices divots left by his fingers and chuckles. Standing Carr can see horseshoe prints in the softening timbers. Midway the third log has split and is sagging, held in place by the old bindings.

Making a mental note he walks on the first two. Hopping off the end he looks back and smiles at the horse tracks left behind.

Pack in place and back in the saddle they carry on. Reaching the campsite within the hour and before the forest becomes black.

Tying the horse to the usual spot Carr notices the swords he poorly crafted are gone.

Picking up wood to start a small fire he studies the small boot prints left behind. It appears a fight did take place, softly laughing at the imagined sight of young boys play fighting.

Sitting in his favorite place watching a small fire he drops the pack and sword. Taking out the meal made for him he leans back and contemplates on his journey and what he'll have to say to his mother. Being gone for more than a week with no real notice he knows she's going to have some well selected words for him.

Chapter Four
Are We There Yet?

"Snap" A branch breaks distant in the trees from the direction they came.

Carr sits up listening, glancing at the fire, figuring if its been seen there's no use putting it out.

Another snap, Carr stays low hiding behind the big rock. Resting one hand on the rock and the other on the ground he closes his eyes to feel the forest floor. Extremely faint singular thumps are sensed by the nerve endings of his fingertips. An unpracticed skill he can't tell what or how many are out there but something is coming.

Not letting his imagination run wild he sits quietly listening, soon hearing the clinking of metal. Sure it's Darvel's men, he thinks hastily deciding to set them up for an ambush.

Taking Lord Piate's sword and dagger, he leaves the closed pack with his long-sword leaning against it.

Stealthy he slips into the brush taking a position behind a large tree. Concealed in the blacken woods he waits for his eyes to adjust and a visual sighting of what's out there.

Sound of hooves are faintly heard then stop. The forest so quiet the falling leaves sound too noisy to hear over.

Carr's night vision starts to work, nowhere near as good as an elf's but enough to make out objects. Locating the path to the clearing he follows it back catching something move. Focusing on the area he sees a two legged armored being sneaking from tree to tree. The silhouette of the helmet confirms his thought, definitely Darvel's men.

Unsheathing the fancy dagger he feels it for balance, good enough to throw, Carr keeps his hand at the ready.

The soldier stops near the clearing surveying the campsite and the surrounding bush. He looks straight at Carr, but can't see him concealed in the darkness.

The man waves his arm high back and forth, signaling his lone mounted comrade to move forward.

Hearing before seeing, the horseman advances with caution. A loaded crossbow in hand the man searches for any suspicious, moving shadows.

The two soldiers meet and whisper to each other, looking but never pointing.

The first man enters the clearing while his mounted partner watches his back. He notices the sword and pack pointing them out.

Walking the perimeter of the tiny clearing to get a better look in the weeds.

Seeing nothing the soldier waves his comrade in.

Carr stays still against the tree watching the pair.

Carr uses the sound of the horse to mask his movements creeping in close.

Entering the clearing the horseman takes notice of the black mare.

Whispering just loud enough for Carr to hear the walking soldier says. "I swear that's that same horse I was going to take in Ingleside."

The bearded horseman replies. "Well Flea, looks like it's yours now."

Nodding, Flea smiles. "Yup. Say Wyme, do you think he's close?"

Wyme replies. "Would you leave your gear and horse behind?"

"No." Flea, now on edge keeps scanning the area. "Whatcha, wanna do?"

Pointing the crossbow at the pack. "If that's full of loot, we take it and the horse to Lahfee and let the Captain decide what to do."

"Okay." Flea bends down. "Shouldn't we hunt the thief down?"

"We're probably in his territory." Realizing the thought the horseman alters the horse's position. "I don't know where we are but I'm sure that was the Gruns river back there. We'll follow it to Lahfee."

Setting the sword aside Flea suggests. "We should follow the river down to Ahn and wait for the Captain and the others."

Noticing the man is about to open the pack Carr gets balanced and ready to spring forward. Silently sliding the short-sword out of its sheath, resting the tip in the ground.

The man's leather covered horse turns sniffing Carr out. Focusing on the horseman's neck Carr cocks his right arm back to whip the fancy dagger.

Opening the pack Flea utters. "It's loaded."

The moment Carr was waiting for distracted the horsemen glances down to look. Letting the dagger fly and not even waiting to see if it connects, Carr jumps up to rush in.

Opening a bag of jewelry Flea's eyes light up, while Carr rushes in. The dagger pierces the back of horseman's neck, causing the man to harmlessly fire the crossbow.

Flea looks up hearing the brush move, his face turns to dreaded surprise, seeing the thief coming at him with short-sword drawn.

Immediately dropping the crossbow the horseman grabs for the blade.

Flea fumbles to stand and draw his sword, Carr tries to run him through. Already off balance Flea falls back against one of the boulders, avoiding the poisoned blade.

The crossbow breaks hitting the ground, as Carr turns studying his opponents.

Foolishly the horseman plucks out and tosses the blade from his neck. Blood spurts from the wound, he tries to clamp it with his hands.

Noticeably shaken Flea attempts to right himself.

Carr targets him quickly thrashing the sword wildly. Managing to avoid the flurry Flea keeps some distance drawing his sword.

Stepping back to wait for the now armed man to strike, Carr sees the Wyme slide off the horse, landing with a thump.

The sight enrages Flea, now on the attack, forcing Carr to fend off a broad-sword with the small blade.

Blocking and dodging Carr gets in the odd slash neither connect until Flea slices upwards.

Carr leans back putting his left arm up. The broad-sword catches his forearm covering tearing it off, leaving a minor cut on the exposed arm.

Carr spins aside as Flea swiftly slashes again. Avoiding the blade, Carr tries to stab him in the back. Flea kicks Carr aside, they turn and square off.

The bearded man sits up frantically searching a satchel for a bandage to wrap his wound.

With no one to guide him and nervous of the close fighting the armored horse backs out of the clearing.

Knowing he's got to out think Flea, Carr decides to fake him out. Thrusting the short blade for the neck Flea slashes upwards attempting to remove Carr's arm. Hopping back briefly to allow the blade to pass Carr jumps forward nailing Flea. As their chests collide Flea stumbles back.

Carr jabs the man several times with the short-sword. Wearing chain-mail under a leather tunic Flea isn't cut. Pushing Carr off, the poisoned blade cuts across Flea's wrist.

Flea swings his heavy blade as Carr jumps aside landing beside the long-sword.

Picking it up in time to defensively cross both blades. Catching Flea's hefty sword between his crossed blades. Carr arches back avoiding the clearly sharp sword.

Pushing off each other they separate.

Sweat and a gapping mouth tell Carr his opponent is tiring of swinging the big sword. A trickle of blood runs down both of their left fingers.

Figuring the poisoned sword is at work Carr sheaths the short-sword. Flea attacks thrusting straight out, Carr pivots deflecting the sword with his trusty long-sword.

Pulling his sword back Flea kicks Carr in side of the thigh moving him away.

Wrapping his neck wound, Wyme calms evaluating the situation. He'd be more confident if his head wasn't so light and his buddy wasn't breathing heavy.

Springing into action Carr slashes at Flea's side, twisting and blocking with his sword the soldier avoids the attack.

Kicking Carr in the ass the man spins his blade chopping down. The blade skips across the back scales of Carr's body armor. Gravity pulls the broad-sword down slicing into the back of Carr's right calf. Snapping the top strap the shin covering, it falls forward flapping in place by its bottom strap.

Finishing the wrap the bearded man watches intently, routing for Flea to connect.

Yelping slightly Carr turns to see Flea's stepping closer swinging the sword to chop down again. Carr moves opposite of the broad-sword's direction, hacking full force on Flea's right hip. Spared by the chain-mail Carr's blade only cuts the man's tunic and bruises the hip.

Swiftly Carr slices upwards cutting off a long lock of hair and knocking the man's helmet off.

Ducking back Flea feebly swings only scratching Carr's armor.

The unattended and frequently disturbed fire is burning out.

Very pale Wyme has fight left and draws a long-sword, starting in. Alarmed there is still two Carr stays defensive blocking and dodging; swords clashing echoes for leagues.

Beginning to wonder if either is really close to death, Carr spots Flea faltering more. Turning remaining energy towards the other man Carr looks for an opportunity to strike, avoiding Flea.

The bearded man thrusts at Carr. Tiring and not thinking Carr bats the sword away with his exposed arm cutting across the top. More focused on the man Carr slashes down cutting through cloth and severing muscles behind the man's knee. Losing stability the bearded man hacks at Carr's side, nicking only scales.

Stepping in and trying to raise his heavy sword high, Flea slows dropping the weapon before collapsing forward.

Wyme tries to stay upright defending Carr's advances bumping into and off the black mare.

Carr saw it coming swinging low for the other leg he connects, gashing the side of the man's knee.

Struggling to stay vertical the man slashes pitifully at Carr. Easily avoided Carr hacks back knocking the man's sword from his loosening grasp.

Knowing death is near the man drops to his knees with head down waiting for a mercy strike.

Carr spares the man further pain switching the long-sword for the short-sword. Plunging it into the man's neck severing the spine with a twist of the blade.

Sliding from the blade the man lands twitching.

The fire goes out leaving Carr in the dark.

Standing still and at the ready Car waits a moment, making sure the fight is over.

Throwing some leaves on the ambers along with sticks and a little blowing the fire lives. Looking about he sees two that won't.

Taking a drink he sits against the boulder tending to his wounds. The arm is bloody but will stop, the gash to his calf won't.

Cleaning off the other man's long-sword he rests the tip on the flames.

Taking off the hanging shin cover Carr removes the boot, pouring blood out.

Gingerly pulling up his pant leg he reluctantly knows the wound needs to be sealed. Being just a leg to him he doesn't want to waste a potion on it. Adding a few bigger pieces of wood he gets the fire hot.

Shortly the blade begins glowing.

Carr stands picking up the sword.

Clenching his jaw Carr slaps the hot sword tip to the wound holding it steady, for what seems like to him an eternity.

Smelling burning flesh he tosses the sword far into the woods and screams out one loud cry.

Dancing around, a couple tears roll down his face.

Wanting to take his mind of the pain he searches the men.

In the end finding little; three gold, eight silver, three copper and a gold ring he adds the items to his pack. Their weapons, not worth carrying, he stashes in the woods. He was about to disrobe them to sell the noisy chain-mail but had an idea.

Making several struggling attempts, Carr hoists the men onto the back of their horse.

Finding leather straps in one of their satchels he binds their feet and hands together in an effort to make sure they stay in place.

Leading the horse out to the main road he points the animal towards Lahfee and slaps its' hind quarters to get the horse moving.

Returning Carr cuts one of the soldier's bandages in half to wrap his forearm cuts. Attempting to determine how long it's been since the sun went down. Sure that the night is more than half over.

Sitting against the boulder with sword across his lap, he focuses on the tiny dancing flames.

Late the next morning Carr wakes seeing blood allover the site.

Cutting down a shrub he sweeps over the area obscuring footprints and spilt blood.

Gathering his things he notices the mare has got her eyes on something. Carr lines up her sight and sees the distant rear end of a herbivore.

Walking the trail back he can see it's one of Darvel's horses tied to a tree.

Reaching the horse Carr unties it thinking of setting him on his way. Changing his mind. "Well if they were going to take my horse, I might as well take this one."

Removing its leather armor Carr sees a nice still young unsound stallion. Tossing all its' tack except the bridal into the brush, Carr takes the reins and leads the horse back.

Hooking the reins onto the mare's saddle he leads them out of the clearing.

Finished dusting away prints, the shrub is tossed far into the weeds.

Getting up into the saddle, he guides the animals out to the main road and south to Ahn.

The day is turning grey but Carr's hoping to be home by night and before rain falls. Actually looking forward to being attacked by his mother's questions and accusations. No more running for a while. His only concern possible soldiers hanging around Ahn.

Finishing the last of the food Violetta left he hears voices on the road around the next turn. The definite high pitches of females, Carr hopes it is Sonja.

Rounding the bend he sees his favorite young lady and her two friends.

A silly grin forms as Carr watches to see how long it takes for them to notice someone's coming and who.

Looking over her shoulder a couple times Doris's sister, Anna sees Carr approaching and points him out to Doris. The girls glance at him then turn back talking to each other.

Carr knows they're trying to figure out who's coming. Anna and Doris look back staring hard, Carr waves, allowing the girls to figure out who it is.

Doris stops causing the other two to turn and stop, they wave back, Carr mainly notices Sonja.

"Good day ladies." Utters Carr reaching them and jokes. "Returning from Lahfee?"

Anna says. "No."

Smiling, Sonja whispers. "Hello Carr."

Doris is the first one to notice. "Where's Bressi?"

Replying Carr sighs. "I lost her in the mountains." He slides off the horse to walk with the girls. "But Violetta picked out the black mare and I found the other one in the forest."

"Found." Doris giggles nudging him "Soldiers from Monsteil were in town yesterday looking for a thief who stole King Darvel's treasure and killed twenty of his men."

The girls look over Carr, noticing the missing coverings and a wrapped arm.

Carr inquires. "Are the soldiers still in town?"

Anna pipes up. "No they left early this morning. Why are you scared?"

"He's not scared." Doris defends Carr. "If he killed twenty, four more should be easy."

Concerned for his soul Sonja inquires looking into Carr's eyes. "You didn't kill all those men? Did you?"

Not wanting to disappoint Sonja, Carr responds calmly. "No, the stories you hear aren't the truth."

"Oh." Sonja contemplates the answer.

Anna boldly asks. "So how many did you kill?"

Doris's curiosity lies elsewhere. "How much treasure did you take?"

Carefully choosing to answer Doris's question Carr shakes the pack. "This is all I took. And it's stuff the tax collector, Lord Pieate was stealing from the King." Wiggling the hilt of the short sword. "And his weapon, while he slept."

"What?" Sonja looks at him in awe. "You were in his bedroom while he was sleeping?"

With a grin Carr proudly says. "Yup."

The girls bored with the village life are intrigued by Carr's latest adventure.

Remembering what he was going after, Doris asks. "Did you find your rings?"

Carr pats his chest where they hang. "Sure did."

Curiosity peaked Doris demands to hear more. "Tell us about it."

Of course he will, but plays secretive, looking about. "If I tell you, you can't tell anyone else."

Younger and smarter Anna suggests looking at his heavy pack. "What will you give us to be quiet?"

Smarter then her Carr replies pointing to the horses. "How about a ride home."

The laziest of the three, Doris utters. "Done."

Not really what she was hoping for Anna inquires. "How about some gold or gems?"

Noticing that comment appeals to Sonja, Carr gives in, stopping the group. "Alright I'll give you the chance to sift through a bag of my choice and each of you can pick one item for themselves."

The girls' eyes light up with curiosity uttering a trio of Okays, causing them to giggle at each other.

Nodding with a raised brow he moves the horses to the road's edge and removes the backpack.

The girls circle around him watching with interest as he opens the pack.

Carr removes the leather sack of jewelry handing it to Sonja to open. The other two seem to vibrate with anticipation waiting for Sonja to open the bag.

Scanning the area for wanderers, soldiers or bandits Carr catches a glimpse of something he rarely sees.

The girl's eyes widen further, as the bag opens.

Anna's look as though they're about to fall into the bag. Anna and Doris's hands dive in pulling out several pieces a time.

Fingering through the bag Sonja watches them.

"Here." Carr suggests to Sonja. "Let me hold it for you." Taking the bag he holds it open while keeping a look out.

The many pieces of gem encrusted jewelry sparkle, form random shafts of sunlight peeking through the forest canopy fascinating the trio.

Anna puts on everything she touches.

Starting a maybe pile in her left hand, Doris evaluates each piece.

Holding up one at a time, to marvel at each piece's unique qualities Sonja takes her time.

It doesn't take long before the bag is half empty and Anna wearing most of it and asks. "We can only pick one?"

Getting tired of holding the bag Carr explains it to her. "One was the deal, you all said okay. Besides you're gonna have to explain to your parents where it came from. And they won't be happy to know."

"Yeah." Doris sighs.

Anna foolishly says. "They don't have to know."

Starting to feel guilty Sonja utters. " I don't know? Maybe I shouldn't."

Not thinking he'd have to talk her into it, Carr makes a suggestion. "Take a piece with lots of gems. Hide it somewhere outside the house and save it."

Anna inquires removing lesser pieces. "Why would we save it?"

Carr puts a question to them. "Do your parents have times where a couple gold could make a difference?"

The young ladies look to each other and nod yes.

"Right." Carr continues with his thought. "Each little gem is worth at least a couple gold. In times of need you could easily pluck a gem out and take it to your parents saying you found it on the road. Or what about later in life when you have little ones of your own and your man has gone off to fight. There will be something there."

Anna and Doris were going to take a piece anyway but wait for Sonja's decision.

Sonja looks to Carr. "You make a good point."

Relieved the girls make their choices discarding the no's back into the bag.

Sonja keeps a bracelet made of seven gold chain chains with gems set into each link, explaining the reasons for keeping it.

Picking between three long necklaces lined with precious stones Doris makes her choice on which one has the bigger centerpiece. Choosing the one having an ornate platinum medallion of a flower with a two hundred gold sized, pink diamond in the middle.

Anna's the heaviest of them, all asking where she's going to hide it. Shrugging she hangs the necklace around her neck made of five jeweled strands and a dozen larger emerald stone pendants hang from it.

Placing the bag back Carr offers. "Would you ladies still like to ride?"

"Okay." Anna says getting on top of the mare.

"Hey." Doris stares hands on her hips at her sister. "I'm not riding bareback."

Carr points out. "There's only two horses. We're going to have to double up."

Sonja notices the rear horse has no saddle and doesn't want to ride bare back either.

Until, Carr happens to add. "Violetta loves to ride bareback and got herself a horse too."

"She probably rides bare skinned too." Doris jests waving at her sister to make room as she puts her foot in the stirrup. "You two can ride together."

Sonja replies with sarcasm. "Thanks." She does respect Violetta and wishes she could heal and birth babies. "Alright I'll try." She looks to Carr. "You'll be a gentleman and if I want down you'll let me?"

A warm smile crosses Carr's lips. "Of course."

He hands the reins to Doris. "Hold him steady."

She nods pulling the horse close to the mare.

Carr assists Sonja to get up and comfortable.

Making a couple of attempts he gets himself up. Taking the reins back Carr nudges the stallion.

Sitting in front of her sister, Anna takes the mare's reins and follows.

As they head south, horses side by side Carr tells them about his journey. Trying to hide his giddiness from being so close to Sonja.

Starting from when they last met, informing them if they had gone to Lahfee that the minstrels had left.

A few, I told 'yous' are uttered and some finger pointing gestures made.

He entertains them with an enhanced version of the fight with the ogre. Knowing these young ladies will talk he leaves out both encounters with Kryston.

Inside the tax building for Sonja's benefit, he only knocks out and tied up the guards. The girls wanted more details on the Lord's bedchambers.

In the cellar there are only the chests locked behind bars. Not interested in the details of lock picking they preferred hearing about the chest's valuable contents.

Playing up the rest of the events into the mountains, where he sent Bressi on her own to mislead his pursuers. Never to be seen from again.

The battle on the mountain stays true but he says he walked to Ingleside collapsing at Violetta's door. She took him in and saved his life, again. The rest stays the same as they near the village.

Doris gets Anna to hide her gaudy necklace and the girls slide off the horses not wanting to be seen entering the village with Carr.

Understanding but disappointed he gets off to help Sonja down.

"Here you go Sonja." Carr smiles at her. "I hope I was gentlemanly enough for you?"

"Yes." Having actually enjoyed the time spent, Sonja thanks him. "Wow Carr I didn't think I was gonna like riding bareback. But I kinda liked it." Out of character she plants a soft kiss to Carr's cheek.

In awe Carr's face turns pinkish as Sonja, a little nervous of her own action runs toward the village.

The sister's also surprised smile and chase after her.

"Thank-you Carr." Sonja calls out running away.

Anna utters a thanks catching up to Sonja.

Doris not really running turns pointing her finger and winking at Carr saying thanks and calling out loudly. "Sonja, likes, Carr! Oooo."

Not sure what to do with himself Carr just ties the horse to the other, watching them.

Back in the saddle he continues on to the village.

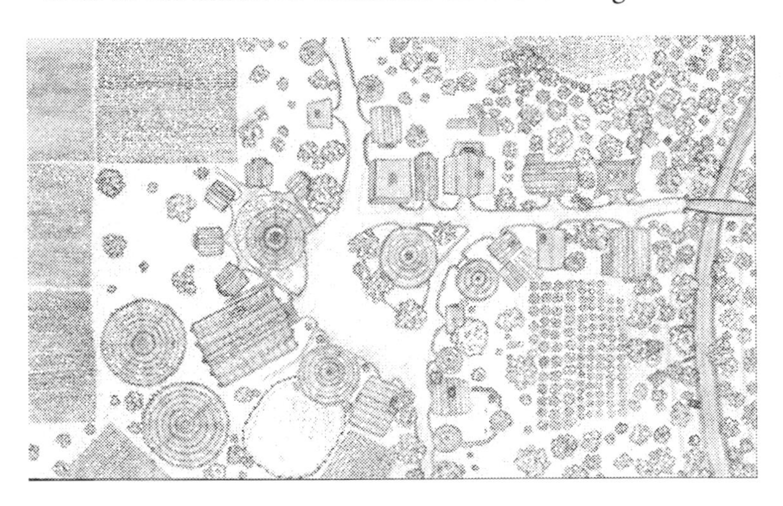

Passing the village fields Carr notices some of the younger men, watching the trio of giggling girls running into the village.

The men don't notice Carr until he passes the first field. Figuring that's what the girls were running from, the men glare at Carr wondering what trouble he's bringing with him.

Passing through the tiny community Carr sees, he's the local source of gossip for the month and sits tall.

Children playing and elders talking stop to check Carr out as he passes. He waves and says hello but gets few replies including one wrinkly finger.

Across the way Effim watches making sure it's him. "Hey! Carr!" The boy runs out barefoot to greet him.

Waving Carr replies. "Hey F! Is your dad home?"

Coming up beside Carr checking out the horses Effim answers. "Yeah he's in the hut. Where's Bressi? And who's, horses are these? Is that my sword?"

"O poor Bressi." Carr informs him. "She's gone. Violetta picked out this one." Patting the horse's shoulder, pointing back. "I found him this morning. The sword is too dangerous for you. I've got to make it disappear."

Disappointed Effim utters. " Ohhh.?!" Checking out the animals. "What? You found a horse?"

Chuckling lightly Carr says. "Yah, he was left tied to a tree. Don't know where his rider could be?"

Hopping on the back of the stallion for a brief ride Effim notes. "You're missing some of your armor."

"Ah it's not missing." Pointing to the pieces dangling from the saddle. "My bow, quiver, sword sheath and saddlebags are missing." Mumbling. "As well as my shirt and cloak."

Hearing the list, Effim offers his services. "I can find you a new cloak and saddlebags. Maybe a sheath. Pa's got arrows and a few bows."

Stopping beside the archer's circular adobe hut Carr slides down, tying the mare to a post. "Well the saddle bags maybe, let's chat with your Pa first."

"Okay." Effim hops off to tie the other horse.

Pulling back the old animal hide that covers the doorway he sees one of his favorite locals.

Off to the side a tall lean elf, human mix, sits binding feathers to a stiff reed shaft.

Effim barges past to announce Carr's presence. "Hey Pa, Carr's here."

The man shakes his head answering. "I knew it to be, when you ran out calling his name." Never looking he continues with finishing the task at hand. "Hey Carr, come on in. Effy hand him his arrows."

Eagerly Effim jumps over to them. "Pa he needs a quiver too. You want me to see if Denko has any?"

"Hold on." Carr calmly speaks taking his pack off. "Let me get some coins." Setting it on the ground he bends down to open it.

Nosey, Effim sets the bundled arrows beside Carr. "Here you go." Then stands close by to see what's in the backpack.

"Thanks guy." Carr opens the cover feeling out the sock of gold. "I'll give you some coins and try and find the things I was looking for."

"Okay." Effim watches intently counting each coin that Carr pulls out.

Thinking about how much he'll need Carr queries. "If he's got saddle bags how much will they cost?"

Effim utters "Five gold." Seeing the coins in hand, he says. "Better get four more for everything."

Giving him a funny look Carr shelters the coins with his fingers thinking about what he said was lost. "Ah, I got the old sheath at home and a shirt isn't that important."

Outstretching his hand Effim says. "Well two more then, Come on let's go."

Chuckling Carr hands him eight gold coins. "You keep what's left."

Being a gold less then what was suggested the young boy stands looking at him. "I'm not haggling for you."

"Alright." Handing him another gold Carr grins.

Pausing at the doorway Effim says to Carr. "But I'll haggle for my gain." Then runs off.

Not really caring Carr bends down to inspect the arrows, asking Hal. "Hey, have you ever heard of a creature called a lammasu."

He nods checking the finished arrow. "Why? Somebody want you to hunt one?"

Examining his new arrows Carr says. "No. Just wanted to know if they are real like some of those myths. Bugs in your eyelashes, yah right."

Setting the arrow aside Hal comments about Effim. "Smartest of all my children and their children. But I think after Claire is gone I'm gonna leave women alone… Well maybe just go after the older ones."

Hal looking the age of a fit man in his forties is one hundred thirty seven. Being a half-breed the elves wouldn't accept him, human women gladly will. Having out lived three of his wives, five children and in the past few years four grandchildren, he feels cursed by his extended life.

Fascinated by Hal's youth and the venture's with his parents, Carr looks up to him lately for advice that a mother can't give. "Yah, he's a good one. So what do you know about lammasusis."

Giving Carr a funny look Hal responds. "I'm not sure what you're up too. But you should leave such creatures alone. They're smarter bigger and faster than you. Not to mention they can tear you apart before you can draw a sword."

Carr accidentally utters. "I'm glad I didn't."

Now interested in what the young rogue has been up too for a week Hal says. "Well go on spill your guts allover the ground. We both know you want to."

Carr leans forward and tells the complete tale as it happened. Hal says nothing, barely moving as Carr even animates the fights.

Making only a dozen embellishments to enhance the story finishing with Effim running to greet him.

Having let Carr ramble Hal questions him. "Your not thinking of giving that poisoned sword to Effim?"

"Oh, no way." Carr digs out the matching dagger handing it to Hal. "I was considering giving him this. I'm gonna hide the short-sword."

After examining the dagger Hal hands it back. "Nice blade. Don't bother Claire would kill us all. You don't live here so you don't hear about it. That Lord Pee stealing, not so surprising but blaming you for taking it all. Geez what nuts he's got."

Putting the dagger away Carr simply agrees. "Yah I know eh?"

Leaning forward Hal tries to scare Carr. "This is what I don't get you made a deal with a beast that uses magic and drinks the blood of it's dying victim and broke it. Aren't you worried he's listening to you right now." He sits back waiting for the look of concern.

"Ah well I didn't ahh.." Carr actually starts looking around worried.

Hal laughs. "Your hilarious, he can't hear us and they're good natured creatures. Normally they avoid us two legged beings." He leans forward inquiring. "So what was it like to fly on his back? I've never gotten the chance to ride any flying beasts."

Carr replays it in his mind, acting it out for Hal going into great detail. "I've never felt anything like it. More exciting than a good fight or even a great hunt. I wish I had wings."

"That's something." Hal is a bit envious of Carr but doesn't show it.

Effim comes in carrying garments. "I put the saddle bags on the black horse." Handing Carr the rest. "I got you a shirt too."

Taking the pile of goods Carr inquires. "So what was your take?"

Smiling wide Effim shakes the coins in his clamped hands. "Ooo just seven silver…And two gold." Taunting Carr.

Pushing the boy's hands aside Carr jokes. "Most capable slave ever. Well worth the money."

Despite being called a slave, Effim is just happy to have for a villager, a lot of money. Showing the coins proudly to his father.

Hal finds them amusing much like siblings. "That's good boy. Cause that's all your mom's gonna let you take from that scoundrel." Pointing to Carr.

"Yeah I know." Effim scuffs the dirt floor. "When's mom gonna let me have a real weapon."

"Hah." Hal breaks the news to him. "Your mom, don't want you touching any weapons. Hell, she says, that's the reason she's gonna live long. To make sure you never can." Pointing at Carr. "And she surely ain't gonna let you travel with him. Especially after you tried following him."

Not offended Carr has already been taken aside by Claire and told the same thing with a few threats tacked on. "Sorry guy your mom threatened us, can't help you." Using Violetta's comments badly. "Get a sickle, they kill too." Setting the pile down.

Just seeing it as a farm tool Effim isn't impressed and asks. "Why are yous afraid of mom? She's little and complains about lifting heavy things. And she don't even use weapons. Just tell her."

For the first time in many years Hal busts out laughing until his belly aches.

Also laughing Carr remembers more of Violetta's wisdom and lists some things for Effim. "Alright, she has a different strength that a good man doesn't want to disturb. Tell me do you like it when she makes you some thing to eat?"

Effim softly utters a restrained. "Yes."

"Do you like it when she takes care of you, when you're sick or hurt?"

"Yes."

"Do you like it when she defends you and yells at the other adults?"

A smile forms on Effim's face again. "Yeah."

Carr can't help but smile back. "How about when she takes you down to the river?"

"Yah."

"And you know no matter how bad you are she's the only one who's gonna love you."

"Yeaahhh."

"So if you want her to always do those things for you. You have to do what she wants." Carr points to his chest. "If you're like me you'll have a mom that's always mad at you."

Still chuckling Hal points out to his son. "You know, she takes you to the river because you stink."

"Yeah but its fun anyway." Effim stands there thinking about what he was told and figures he's got all he could out of Carr this time, saying. "I think mom said she needed help."

Hal nods. "Yeah boy why don't you, she'll need wood a think."

Leaving Effim notes. "Hey an axe is a weapon."

Carr utters. "Makes you stronger too."

"Violetta." Hal smiles. "If I hadn't met Claire… She's a good woman, too good for the likes of us. Is that where you got that stuff from?"

"Yup." Carr sighs agreeing with him. "She's told me over and over."

Hal reaches back and picks up his latest creation. "Have I got a bow for you to try." Handing the bow to Carr, he stands to retrieve a couple target arrows.

Carr examines the bow and notices something unusual. "Hey is this made from wood strips?"

"Sure is." Hal motions Carr to follow him out the back opening."

Following Carr asks. "Isn't it going to crack?"

"It's similar to how the elves craft their bows. I can't recall the wood that they used but I found some maple that certainly worked."

Still studying it Carr sees the bindings but no visible separations. "How's it staying so tightly together?"

"That's why this bow is yours for free." Hal hands him the arrows pointing out his new straw target. "You left that container of really sticky goo. Ah, you said from some alchemist. Anyway it was perfect."

Liking the look of the bow Carr readies an arrow and aims down range. "Hey, nice target looks kinda like a person made of straw."

Hal points out. "Effim's idea he asked if I could hit an apple in his hand. His mother over heard and voiced her opinion." Pointing to the target. "So we put that together. Effim calls it the Straw King."

Carr lines up the arrow to roughly where a heart should be. "The draw doesn't seem any different."

"Wait until you let go." Hal watches Carr's form.

Carr releases the arrow, it sails noticeable faster diving into the straw target exactly where he was aiming. "Impressive."

Drawing back the second arrow. "Better make sure that wasn't a fluke." Carefully aiming and releasing the arrow, it penetrates the dummy next to the first.

Holding up the bow Carr glances at Hal. "This is great can't wait to try it on something moving."

Nodding Hal informs him. "Those different pieces give it more spring. There's enough of that goo to make a few dozen bows. And small critters don't stand a chance against skilled bowman."

Larger critters interest Carr. "How about bear?"

"Now don't get foolish." He thinks of something it might take down. "Maybe a big buck. Or ogre."

Grinning at the new toy, Carr says. "Thanks Hal I'll certainly put it to the test." Sliding it around his body he notices the sun has started its' decent. "I suppose, I best get moving again."

Hal takes a look too. "Yah you should make it home by nightfall."

Entering the hut, Carr organizes his gear talking to Hal. "Did you, happen to check in on Ma for me?" Holding the oversized shirt up to his chest.

"Wear it as a cloak." Hal comments. "Yes I did, after a little fishing at the swamp. Dirtied up your bed for you. She doesn't seem too mad, this time."

Placing the bundled arrows into the new leather quiver. "Thanks I appreciate that." Carr studies the detail work. "For an old guy he's getting better. I like the darker hides."

Hal checks it out. "I think this is the work of his granddaughter." Nodding he confirms the thought. "She's nine and is always in his shadow."

About to close up the pack Carr inquires. "Did you want anything from here? Several platinum, some gems? Or pearls."

"Nah?" Having seen too many killed over a silver Hal has little interest in wealth. "You'll need more than that to build your castle."

Checking once more Carr asks differently. "Something for a birthday or anniversary."

That catches Hal's ear. "Well that would be an idea now. You got some simple pieces so she doesn't ask too many questions."

Carr hands him the bag of jewelry. "Well have a look. While I put some of this stuff on the horse." Leaving Hal to sift through it.

Out front the village is getting quiet as the field workers return home to dine. By the scented smoke wafting from Hal's house chimney, food is cooking.

Carr checks out the space inside the saddlebags, not as big as the old one but made from the same hide as the quiver.

After stuffing his new cloak and shirt in, Carr affixes the quiver and bow to the other side catching a glimpse of Claire overseeing him.

Waving to her, she slyly smiles erecting a finger to wave back.

Dropping his head and sighing he returns inside the hut. "Well Claire's not furious, with me."

Holding out two elegant gold chain necklaces Hal tries to determine which pendant she'd like better. "I take it she was watching you."

"Oh yah." Carr tucks the bag into the pack.

Hal says. "I still have one."

Closing the lid Carr tells him. "They're both nice. So, whichever one you don't want, I'll surprise Ma with in the winter. For her birthday."

"Smart thinking." Making his choice Hal hands the other to Carr. "Thank you, this'll get me some lovin."

Getting the pack and sword in place Carr says. "I'm sure it will." Patting the rings under his plate. "I hope these will keep me from being chewed out."

"I'm sure they will." Hal hides the necklace high in the straw roof of the hut. "Claire never comes out here. Someday she won't be so mad with you. It takes her a long time for her to get over things. She still reminds me, the day I called her by the wrong name."

"Oh yah." Carr's heard the story. "While you were being married." Carr shakes Hal's hand. "Good luck with that one. And thanks again for everything."

"No worries, glad to help." Hal walks him to the horses. "Say hello to your mum too."

Carr hooks the reins of the stallion to the saddle. "I will and stop around next time your near."

Hal checks out the horses uttering. "Usually do."

"Nice eh?" Untying the mare Carr comments. "Is Claire ever gonna let Effim go bow hunting?"

"Ssshhh" Hal hushes Carr. "I'm waiting for her annual decision. I don't want anything to sway her."

"Sorry." Carr whispers, getting into the saddle. "I'll be glad to be dumping this stuff off soon."

"I would be too." Hal rounds the stallion. "These are good animals. Do they respond well?"

Carr nods. "Well I can't say for certain about the stallion but this mare does." He pats the horse's side, directing her to the road. "See you next time."

Waving slightly Hal replies. "I hope the road home is quiet." Turning he heads into the house to see what's cooking.

Carr and the horses head south down his most familiar road acting as guide and sage. Informing the horses about their new home territory.

Showing them one of the last surviving Ebony trees, Carr notices the mare's ears perk up.

Wondering if he's found a name she'll respond to, Carr leans forward. "Eeboony, Oh Ebony."

She turns her head back to look at Carr, making him happy and it sounded like a good name.

He thinks of animals he went chasing after that wouldn't listen. Hal told Carr it's because they don't like the name they're given.

Looking back at the stallion Carr's unsure naming different trees and plants. The horse never pays him any mind Carr wonders if the animal might be deaf.

Bored and nervous over what's going to happen when he walks through the door, Carr rambles the rest of the trip away.

With barely a bird to be seen they turn down the obscured path to the farm.

Stopping half way Carr dismounts and leads the horses off the path tying Ebony to a sapling.

Slipping into the old forest he heads west.

Clearing the front section of brush Carr only has wild roots to deal with, as the forest floor is barren of overgrowing vegetation.

After a half a league of walking Carr reaches a wide patch of tall shrubs interlaced with a large leafed vine.

Removing his long-sword he pushes it waist height, through the shrub's many thorn, covered branches. The sword scrapes along the top of a stone-wall, inside the shrubbery.

Cautiously inserting his hands and arms in.

Spreading his arms out as far as the thorny shrubs will let him he eases his way in. Wishing to have at least refitted the left forearm cover.

He sits on a wide ledge of a deep well, picking all the thorns from the arm.

Seeing the way, he hangs his feet over the edge.

Carefully positioned holes and spikes in the well's stonework aid Carr's descent.

After clearing all the cobwebs and upsetting many multi-legged critters, Carr hits the bottom.

Pulling back a filthy blanket with critters of its own, he reveals a beautifully engraved, rusty, iron chest. Opening the unlocked lid, he removes the venomous sword and stores it with several other small bladed weapons. Closing the lid he picks it up and moves it aside.

Underneath a blanket so filthy it doesn't even feel like blanket, pulling it aside.

Resting the pack atop the chest Carr pushes away the moist soil uncovering a buried and rotting barrel.

Removing the lid Carr can't see inside but knows there's several sacks down there with all kinds of small things he's pilfered.

Opening the pack Carr takes a handful of assorted sized gems and places them in his coin pouch adding the loose coins as he finds them. Taking the sacks, bags and socks he makes sure they're secure and drops them in the barrel.

Keeping everything else including the fancy dagger Carr returns things, to the way it was.

A light pack allows Carr to swiftly scale the well.

Exiting the thorny shrubs Carr stops to reposition the branches with his long-sword and uses it again walking back to the horses.

Finding the horses right where he left them he finishes the last league of riding, feeling satisfied with the way things went overall.

Entering the large clearing Carr sees a light on in the kitchen window of the farmhouse. Smoke gently puffs out of the chimney.

Looking to the fields he sighs knowing tomorrow he needs to start taking it down. The same with the backfield, at least the corn can wait a couple weeks.

Keeping an eye on the window for a small silhouette Carr quietly guides the animals to the barn.

On the ground Carr opens the gate to the corral leading the animals to the water trough.

As they drink he removes their tack, stowing it in the barn.

Deciding to ditch his armor before he goes in. Carr quickly removes it putting on his new over sized shirt.

After stuffing his new cloak into the backpack, Carr slings it over his shoulder.

Picking up a sack of animal feed Carr cuts it open, then dumps it near the horses.

Patting them both Carr points to the barn. "Well, Ebony and friend welcome to your new home. Try and make yourself comfortable."

Latching the gate the last rays of light disappear, Carr turns facing the farmhouse taking a deep breath he heads in.

Knocking at the door while opening it. "Hello. It's me Carr returning. Should I just sleep in the barn?"

A small woman, of fifty years, stands off to the left in the kitchen waiting to see how he enters and with what. "Finally decided to come home eh?"

She sees his armor is off and he's got a new shirt on and speaks sternly. "What's the matter soldiers chasing you and you have no place to hide?"

He enters, carefully closing the door. "No."

"Off hunting with Hal you try and tell me?" She speaks in a manner that lets Carr know she's unhappy with being deceived.

Crossing her arms she continues. "Out stealing again. Or fighting." Se points a finger at him. "I can smell the blood on you. You know a bath won't kill you. Or must it be dangerous for you to do it." Shaking her head in disgust.

Listening Carr sets the pack down by the table taking a seat, answering quietly. "I'll do something about that tomorrow."

Ma is just getting started, raising her voice. "And you wasted a bag of feed on those horses." Looking into his eyes. "Where's yours? Did you sell Bressi?"

Not wanting to answer that yet Carr sighs. "No, I didn't sell her. Those animals hadn't eaten in awhile. We've got plenty of food anyway."

She starts pointing at him. "Your aura is all messed up on your left side, and it's more than just your forearm. Isn't it?"

Carr shows her the nasty burn on his calf.

The wound makes her stomach uneasy. "You should let Violetta take a look at that."

Speaking without thinking Carr utters. "She took care of a worse wound."

Her face turns red, trying not to blow up before she can find out what happened. "You had a worse wound than that? I don't even wanna know."

Carr attempts to calm her. "Everything's gonna be okay. I'm not going anywhere. I'll take the fields off. Later we can go to the city and get the supplies we need for the winter."

That comment angers her. "Don't! You dare. Don't even. Just like your father. You'll find something to go chasen. And what is gonna happen is your death. Someday, somewhere for something that doesn't belong to you."

Carr says what needs to be said. "I'm truly sorry. I'm sorry I take off for weeks at a time and don't tell you. And this time I understand how short my life could be if I don't stop."

That she's been waiting years to hear, from all the men in her life. The only sound heard for the next minute is the crackling of the fire.

While she composes herself fighting back tears of frustration she pours out two cups of warm tea and sits across from Carr sliding him one.

Talking a calming sip she says. "Your soon to be a man I can't stop you. But I don't want you here if all you're going to make me do is worry. I don't expect you to stay on the farm forever. But I'd like your help here until I'm gone. If you want to run off and get killed just let me know where you'll be or at least when you'll be back."

Keeping eye contact Carr says. "I'll do right by you Mom. Even this stupid quest was for you."

"What.?!" She becomes agitated again. "Don't you use me as an excuse to get yourself killed." Annoyed she wants to back away from the table.

Carr reaches over and gently grabs her hand. "Wait Ma. Please." Pulling his necklace pouch out.

More curious she stays in place breaking the contact. "What's this, than?"

Seeing he's got a captive audience Carr drops the rings into palm swiftly making a fist before she can see them. "I wanted to make sure these stayed with their rightful owner."

Noticing she's waiting to see, he holds the fist close to her, hovering slightly over the table. Delaying the release for effect.

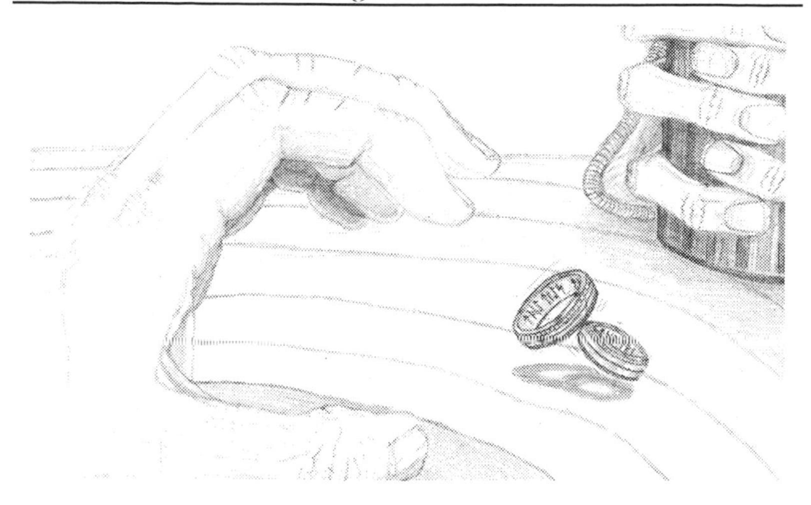

Opening his fingers they fall, she sees two plain silver rings and starts to get mad at the idea of him risking life and limb for that.

Carr watches her face as the rings bounce a couple times of the hard wood surface and begin to spin in small circles. As they slow down she knows, what those rings are and to whom they belong.

As her eyes redden and well up she struggles to speak over whelmed with emotion. "You, these, these are my wedding rings." Her hand quickly goes up to hide her quivering chin. "You, you went to get these back for me."

Carr sits beside her. "Yes Mom that's what I was after." He puts his arm around her.

She grabs the rings up to make sure they're real then pulls them to her chest letting the tears flow.

"Oh Mom." Holding her tight he explains. "I couldn't let them become lost in King Darvel's treasure vaults. Besides the farm, that's all you have left of Dad's. If we had to flee here you can't take the farm with you."

She buries her head into his chest. "They're not worth risking your life over. But my heart thanks you."

She sniffs wiping away the tears. "Wait a moment." She sits up starring at him. "Did you break into the same building your father did?"

Carr hopes the worst is over. "Yah, I did."

Getting serious again and cuffing him upside the head she utters. "You broke into King Darvel's property. Risking our life. And all you got out of it was these rings. What the hell's the matter with the you.?!"

"No, no." Carr cuts her ranting short, pulling out his coin pouch. " I took these too." He empties the contents on the table.

She pushes the stones around looking unimpressed. "That's not much for what should have been there."

Carr gives his head a shake in disbelief. "Well I had to get a new horse and tack. Food, lodging plus some healing and purchased some vials of healing."

She had a hunch before but she knows for sure her boy has a stash somewhere. "Well you really shouldn't be doing these things." She gets up kissing his fore head and fixes him a simple meal.

Hoping the emotional storm, has subsided, Carr restates his intent. "I'll start on the fields in the morning. When they're off we'll go to the city. After that we'll be stuck together until spring."

Setting a couple baked meat and vegetable rolls down for Carr she pokes him. "So out with it you must be aching to tell your story."

Stories with his mother always take longer being filled with questions and comments most of the time it annoys him except for today. While eating Carr starts from when he left.

She already starts. "I knew before I got back."

"I'm sure you did." He tells her about seeing Sonja passing through Ahn

"That's what you need a nice woman to raise a family with, that's plenty of adventure."

"So I keep hearing." Animating the part of racing blindly through the Tau woodlands in a thunderstorm.

She informs him. "Those woods are dangerous around there."

"Yes so are the low hanging branches." He starts to tell her about the ogre.

"I told you those woods are dangerous."

"Anyway.." Carr knows she doesn't care for swordplay and keeps it short. When he gets to Kryston he tells her the truth not getting far.

"A lammasu, what the hell were you thinking. You shoulda gotten out of there."

"Do you want to hear?" He asks. Seeing her nod he briefly continues.

"You made a deal with a beast?"

"Yes Ma can I continue? I am still alive."

Motioning him to go on, he does. She manages to listen for a while. In this version he simple scales the building, sneaking pass the roof top guard. Knocking out the upper floor guard and to keep it simple he tells her the rings were found in Lord Piate's closet chest.

"You know what I think. I think that Lord Piate is stealing from the King."

"Me too Ma. Me too." He says he just slipped out the back doors and went on about the strange innkeeper.

"She's probably a witch. After your soul."

"Ma I'm still here." He chuckles continuing, she follows along until he nods off in the clearing.

"You can't go to sleep while being chased."

"Well I did and I got caught." Describing the conversation with the men and his hasty escape.

"It's not safe in that part of the range at night."

Carr sighs. "I've been told." Just giving her the basics of the fight and what happened after.

She stays quiet but the bringing up the second meeting with Kryston.

She has to say. "You made another deal.?! With a beast, who ate your horse?"

"Yes Ma. I was bleeding to death. And he got me to Ingleside after midnight."

She curiously asks. "How did this beast get you from the mountains to Ingleside so quickly?"

Grinning Carr tells her. "We flew."

"You, What?! Flew?" She's not sure how to react to that but having never flown herself inquires. "What was it like?"

Telling it better the second time Carr animates it again using his bed as the mountain and the table as Ingleside. "O Ma, there's nothing I can compare it to." He sits down going over the events in town.

"Did you tell Violetta I said Hello?"

Stopping Carr cold. "Ingleside…Well, maybe. I know I invited her for a visit. Anyway…" Returning to his tale becomes difficult.

With every few sentences she makes a remark, Carr reluctantly answers. She even has something to add as leaves Ingleside.

Ma kindly suggests. "You know Violetta loves you like a little brother. She just wants you to stay alive too. And you should show her better respect."

Carr huffs once. "I know Ma…" Thinking of something his mother will say no to. "…Hey why don't we take some of the crops to sell in Ingleside we'll pay Violetta a visit."

"That'd be nice." She says at first. "But I don't like that town. It's too far."

Rolling his eyes Carr proceeds getting as far as the make shift bridge. Where she bores him with the same old stories. The actual troll who built it just because of the tales. That's where her and his father, Alfred use to hide away to, as early teens. The poor kids, who drowned diving off it.

Where he informs her of the horse knocking him off leaving shoe prints behind. She laughs and harder after he tells her about the finger divots left.

Snickering and disappointed he didn't hit water she jests. "You needed a good cleansing anyway."

Finding it amusing Carr smiles, replaying the events of last night. Not at all thrilled in the killings of more soldiers her face goes cold. Well use to that face he informs her that's where the other horse came from.

Her interest returns with the reappearance of Sonja but stays quiet, hoping to hear something good. Carr alters the storey slightly from giving them jewelry to just a gem. Foolishly brining up the thank you she gave brings questions.

"She Kissed you.?!" A mother asks nosily concerned. "Where? If her parents find out they'll take her away. In my day we'd have to marry if caught."

Carr plays difficult jumping to the next part. "You'll never guess…Who came out running to greet me. Effim."

A topic his mother is fond of, little Effim and his attractive father. "Effim? He must be getting big."

"He is and smart like a sage." Carr replies telling her about being taken by him.

She laughs again, agreeing with Carr's statement. They sit and talk into the night about Hal. The old days when he, Alfred, and her were out reeking havoc on the world. The stories Carr loves to hear and motivated him into the foolhardy quests taken.

THE END (of that ride)